PROPERTIES OF LIGHT

REBECCA GOLDSTEIN

PROPERTIES OF LIGHT

❖ ❖ ❖ ❖ ❖ ❖ ❖ ❖ ❖ ❖ ❖ ❖ ❖ ❖ ❖ ❖ ❖ ❖

A NOVEL OF LOVE,

BETRAYAL

AND QUANTUM PHYSICS

HOUGHTON MIFFLIN COMPANY
BOSTON • NEW YORK

Library of Congress Cataloging-in-Publication Data

Goldstein, Rebecca, date.
Properties of light : a novel of love, betrayal and
quantum physics / Rebecca Goldstein, date.
    p.   cm.
ISBN 0-395-98659-1
1. Quantum theory — Fiction.
2. Physicists — Fiction. I. Title.
PS3557.O398 P76 2000
813'.54 — dc21 99-049994

Printed in the United States of America

QUM 10 9 8 7 6 5 4 3

FOR MYNDA AND RENA

SOURCES OF LIGHT

ACKNOWLEDGMENTS

I am grateful to the Bogliasco Foundation, which allows artists and scholars of various disciplines to tarry a brief while on the Italian Gulfo di Paradiso, where much of this novel was conceived.

I am also extremely grateful to the MacArthur Foundation. It was only that shockingly unexpected phone call that made it possible for me to write again. Like so many others, I am deeply indebted to Joel Lebowitz.

I have recently become blessed with an agent, Tina Bennett, of uncommon multiple talents, and with Elaine Pfefferblit, who has been all that one could desire in an editor.

Once again, thanks must go to my daughters, Yael and Danielle, always my first, and kindest, readers. This novel grew out of a bedtime story I told Danielle one night some years ago.

My deepest gratitude is reserved for Sheldon Goldstein, whose passion for science and truth has always taught me much, and inspired me still more.

Then tell me, what is the material world,
and is it dead?

— WILLIAM BLAKE

PROPERTIES OF LIGHT

I

The essential fact is that I hate her.

My hatred is my cause: material, formal, final. It makes my world for me. I have largely forgotten the feel of things unimplicated in its being. For them, I retain only the words, as empty as plundered graves. The diminishment bothers me less than I would have imagined, there remaining still so much to me, to the substance of my thoughts, the implications of my hatred being many.

Such hatred as mine might be described as obsessive, although the description would be false. Would an obsessive even pose the possibility of his own delusion? The stance of objectivity required in order to ask of oneself whether one is obsessing is unassumable for those who, in fact, are.

This is my first argument.

Does it lead to a more general result, namely that the answer to the question *Am I obsessing?* must be a logically certified *no?*

As a matter of fact it does. This is interesting, though not very. I have not produced, by any stretch, a result remotely on the scale of the sublime Descartes's analogously conclusive remarks concerning the question *Am I existing?* Formally, my argument and his share this feature: the very conditions that must hold in order for the question to be put at all determine its answer. In the case of the Cartesian question, the answer is affirmative, and metaphysics has produced, in the four hundred years since, nothing much better than this. It is not only interesting but supremely practical. What could be more useful than having the means of convincing oneself that one exists whenever the question should arise? Without it, I might degenerate into a very dubious modality of mind. I might go mad.

Here is my second argument, and it, too, is faintly redolent of the subtle rationalist. There is an affinity almost natural between the Cartesian condition and me. My second argument: Obsession connotes excess, and excess, in turn, unnecessity. If my hatred is obsessive, then it must be possible for me to exist, at least in principle, without it. And yet of all I once thought true of me, it is my hatred alone that cannot be separated from me. Of all else I know I can be deprived and still continue to be, since of all else I have in fact been deprived. But of my hatred? It might possibly be the case that if I ceased entirely to hate that I should likewise cease altogether to exist.

I am a real thing and really exist, but what thing? I have answered: a thing that hates.

My indifference to the world at large is absolute. Outside of my hatred, I care not what exists, nor how, nor why. Properties of matter and energy, of space and time? Less real to me now than the unseen object is said to be to the newborn tabula rasa. No pull left in these subjects to keep me put, I glide off.

I glide away.

My almost universal indifference is all the more remarkable considering that I am, by training, a physicist, once said by some (most certainly by me) to have inhabited a singularity of promise. I might have been expected to preserve some lingering interest in the ultimate constituents of existence. I have none. Were an angel of God to offer me the definitive description of the properties of light (for it was on them and their paradoxical duality, both wave- and particlelike, that my singularity of promise had once largely been focused) I doubt I'd even hear the cherub out. I can attend to nothing but the essential fact, its decoherent history, configurations traced impermanently among ill-defined confusions. One might have thought that I'd know more, one might have thought.

It is a warm night and windless. The air hangs still and

heavy. One feels that one might float on it, as on a waveless sea. Above, the moon is hanging low, like a puckered-up bulge of a belly.

That was a repulsive simile.

I once thought that darkness was as real as light, was even more real. I figured darkness to be not the absence of light, but rather light the absence of darkness.

I was an inveterate and inventive theorizer as a child. Instinctively, I read the observable world as a system of coded signs. My theory of darkness was one of my earliest juvenilia, dating from a time while I still lived in the haze of unbroken-in consciousness. I had (still young) to discard it, however, for as a theory it had a flaw: it was untrue. Light is the something, and darkness its privation. I can no longer remember the precise reasoning that led to my rejecting the primacy of the dark. The distinction between truth and falsity has always mattered much to me.

A warm night and windless. Summer nights have qualities hospitable to habitations, by old memories and the like, all manner of insinuations carried weightless in thin air. A quiet night steeped deep in summer, yielding itself to all manner of insubstantialities, desires perfectly preserved in the bitterness of mind.

There are others I could hate as well, with all my soul, as I hate her, and yet I don't. My hatred, though essential, is essentially of her, and, in that sense, external. I was not a hating child. Hatred requires an attention that it was not yet in me to squander on people. I had other things to think about. So far as people were concerned, I was largely not concerned, with the sole exception of Jake Childs, who was my father, and Cynthia Childs, née Rosenthal, who was my mother. The world for me was fixed around them, and there was nothing in it for me to hate.

My parents and I were, from as far back as I remember, the best of chums, composing a perfect Platonic solid, so that the running commentary of my contemporaries — *nerd! geek!* — sounded faintly, like some far-off phantom choir. I suppose I was a nerd and geek, too nerdy and geeky to care. I think the words hardly signified at all. We were what we were, we three, with neatly overlapping interests: my father and I in abstract argument; my mother and I in beauty; my father and mother in me. We all understood one another with a perfect accord, which would have been as gratifying for a well-disposed outsider to observe as would his observance be disruptive of the very state to be observed.

This is a nuisance very central to modern physics.

It was a touchingly typical boyhood, *mutatis mutandis,* of course, for it is true that at an age when my contemporaries were having their this-little-piggy-wiggies wiggled, I was solemnly reciting the law of the excluded middle — *every statement is either true or false, and no statement is both!* — and constructing truth tables for propositions of first-order logic. And nights, it is true, would never find the three Childses — Papa Childs, Mama Childs and Baby Childs — huddled around the softly glowing television sets whose jumpy phantasmata were thrown off flickering from the windows of our neighbors. We owned no television but sought what spectacles we craved from the nighttime skies. It was our habit to arrange ourselves on our backs in our modest and mythical backyard, studiously murmuring, even in the chilly seasons lying on the unmade lawn and staring up at softly glowing galaxies, inhabiting a space measured out in units of time, delivered by the speed of light. My mother, her daytime diffidence shed beneath the stars, fingered constellations and supplied the ancient myths to go with them.

And yet, as these things go (they go, they go), we were not, after all, so very different from the huddling masses. Papa Childs, Mama Childs, Baby Childs: we were quite as safe as truth by convention could make us.

I have always lived in academic towns. My childhood home, white on the bottom, with green bumpy shingles on the top, was located in an academic town. It was called *Olympia*, so that we were, one and all, *Olympians*.

This is also an academic town, very famous, perversely high-toned. It is where she lives, the reason that, expressly unbidden, I have nevertheless come. Just for the moment I have forgotten its name, the emptied sound has slipped my mind. The stars are threshed, and the meanings are threshed from their husks. It will return to me shortly, the name of this place.

It is far quieter here in the summer than in the other seasons. Unburdened of its students, the university assumes its ideal form. In the silence before dawn, I have the campus to myself, no fear that I will suddenly be confronted by glassy-eyed youths, stinking from the quantities of drink and animal spirits in them. I am exquisitely sensitive to smells. The earth is a swarming confusion of scents, and quite a few of them are noisome.

The asphalt paths that crisscross the grassy lawns have gone a mercurial gray and slick with moon. I wander them to all my favorite haunts. It is said to be a beautiful campus, and even I now find it so. It is very beautiful to me.

When I first came here I had no eye for it, for beauty of its kind, gloomy and Gothic and grand. The massive stone and vaulting towers. They diminished me to near extinction. I hate it, quite generally, when matter presumes.

Now, though, I am very changed, and wind my way with something like love past the castellated undergraduate dorms, whose shady courtyards are special favorites of mine. A pool of water catches a fleeting glimpse of moon and me and ripples softly, water against stone.

There is a wooden swing that hangs from a long and yellow braided rope, like Rapunzel's plaited hair, an enchanted ladder a prince might scramble up to find his pleasure.

So let me find my pleasure.

The swing moves slightly as I pass, its slow creak trailing after me as I cross the street that once formed the natural boundary of the university, which has now been pushed outward by the vigors of the natural sciences and the other well-endowed departments.

The physics complex, its utilitarian thrust a contrast to the flushed romanticism of the older campus, is being added onto once again, bricks and mortar waiting on the shrinking polygon of lawn, for the funds keep pouring in, converging here like moths to light. It is a celebrated faculty, more so now than ever, three Nobel immortals and seven MacArthur geniuses, this grand university's most grand and favored spot. I can rarely return, but I must stop and stare awhile at the austere structure wherein the labyrinthian physics of the day is made.

I once was a physicist. I had my place here in this world. I was given an office up on the seventh floor, the starry seventh, where the brightest stars are constellated.

It would not surprise me in the least if there were souls within as sleepless as I, even now, at this unpeopled hour, pacing the hallways in feverish cerebration, launching tenuous calculations into the well-kept mysteries of matter's true nature. Some graduate student, perhaps, or very junior faculty member, too alone to have any idea of how lonely he is, as I, too, used to work my way straight through to the first light, astonished to look up and discover that it was dawn.

It's best like this, with the dormitories emptied, the rowdy routed, the vacuous evacuated. (I have become a phrase-maker. I have the time.) Those who remain can hear themselves think, as I hear myself think, as I am thinking even now, if you can call this *thinking*, if you can call this *now*.

The passage of time is nothing real. It is a chimera spun out of gauzy consciousness, and nothing more, a frightful apparition tossed up by our mixed-up minds. We know this from Einstein's physics, which shows us a time as stilled as spread space. Time is static, the flow unreal: it is Einstein's truth, and it *is* the truth, falling straight away from the conditions of perfect symmetry imposed on the geometry. The ebb, which seems so terrible and real, which seems to carry off one's every treasure, leaving one like a chest spilled open on the waves: unreal, unreal.

On Saturdays in winter, which in upstate New York are long and hard and character-enhancing, my father and I would take from their peg on the wall in the "mudroom" (for so we called it) the antique wooden skis that he and his older brother, Freddy (killed in a world war I can now no longer name — the first, the second, the third), had used as boys, and head for the gentle hills of Olympia's country club.

The change of season enmagicked the golf links, expunging all traces of the pampered scampering after the battered balls of summer. (I have the time.) The transformation rendered these our very own Elysian Fields, recast in winter light, the smell of snow on sugar pines, and my father and I, otherwise ill at ease in our long and graceless bodies, were here become as gliding gods.

Within a copse of sheltering pines, we unpacked the ambrosial bologna and mustard sandwiches, slightly crunchy with crystals of ice. The sweetness of hot cocoa that poured out of the red-and-green plaid-patterned thermos into the red plastic cup that cunningly unscrewed from its top derived some portion of its sublimity from the touch of its heat on frozen lips and cold-parched gullet. These were sensations of the body I can recall with perfect clarity and calm. Exquisite pleasures, yet with no a posteriori retchings of the soul. While we ate, we put aside our shared passion for abstraction and produced only such utterances as applied to the progress of our pleasures. "Another sandwich, son?" "Cocoa's gone."

And so, sustained on ecstasy, my father and I would return to the white music of our glissandos, until the early-falling dusk turned the silvery landscape into lead and revealed the cruel edge in the cold.

With something of the godlike still clinging to our forms, we would tramp through the doorway of our little boxy house, my boyish cheeks a burnished tingle, the strange buoyancy associated with the earlier phases of exhaustion floating my arms and my legs.

There would be my mother, her heavy black-framed glasses steamed to white opacity above the trapezoid inscribed between her nose and lips, her two nonslender hands reaching out to me the cup of perfect cocoa, mounded with the sheen of the glarey ethereality known as Marshmallow Fluff. We were very fond in my family of Marshmallow Fluff, a versatile foodstuff that could even serve, when combined with peanut butter between slices of bread, as a main course. The recipe came helpfully printed on the label, on which it was dubbed a *pfeffernuss*. This was, I believe, my first foreign word, spoken before the age of two. How exquisitely incongruous it must have sounded trickling off my infant tongue, and how my parents must have gloated in the love of precocious me, they did, they did. It is an item in my master list of facts.

Winter has always seemed to me to be the time of our greater undiscontent. Our desires contract with the mercury.

Even rapists are appeased. Summer is the ravishing season, releasing the unstaunchable longings. Desire rises up like lubricious water, up, up, and over your head. Learn to breathe it or you drown, alone, alone, your scream unheard.

It is summer now.

It was a blessedly uncomplicated boyhood, as dull as doughnuts. I possessed precisely the blunted consciousness that a child ought to have. Subtlety did not come naturally to me. It is suffering that has tenderized me, pounded me like a piece of choiceless meat. The world, to the child that I was, seemed as straightforwardly self-evident as my meticulously constructed truth tables; no counterfactuals to wreak upon us of regret and longing. There are no Proustisms hulking here on my memory's floor, embedded like an anchor, to be yanked up by a taste. Marshmallow Fluff plumbs no sunken depths.

I come to know of Proust by way of my mother. Each year she reread the entire seven volumes of *À la recherche du temps perdu*. It was a habit that made my father and me intensely proud. *Who do you think her favorite writer is?* he would ask people who had only just met her.

Little boys are said to think their mothers beautiful, but I could never bring myself to discern the traces of a beauty that was not there, the difference between truth and falsity having always mattered much to me. Mixed in among the sheet music, from which she and my father played their duets for euphoniums, were a few pictures of her as a girl, looking earnest, fat and sad.

Her coarse, dark hair, striped wide with white, was cut in the same blunt style as the full-cheeked girl in the photos, with bangs arranged ruler-straight across her forehead. There were two vertical grooves set deep down between her brows. They were like the tracks left by my wooden sled in the snow, as if her soft wad of a nose had slid down her face until it finally caught like a rudder on a hidden tree root and stayed put. When I told her this she laughed, while simultaneously two fingers flew up to trace the lines that she had probably never noticed for herself. She was not a student of her face. She had no vanity. She had a girlish voice, though, a shy and girlish smile. Her laughter was beautiful. A substratum of startled gratitude lay permanently beneath her and spread upward into all her gestures. This gave her sweetness.

A supremely American boyhood, *mutatis mutandis,* as idyllic as if by design. They both died when I was nineteen and a half. A drunk driver came hurtling out of a hidden chaos to fling them out of our shared life and into cold infinity. I was, by no design, an orphan, alone, alone, the cruel edge in the cold a permanent fixture.

Was it called a *pfeffernuss?* Was it? This is the word that comes to mind, but it makes no sense, and how am I to know, *to verify and know?*

They were returning home from a concert of chamber music presented by the faculty of the music department at the small college in upstate New York where my father taught the impossibility of metaphysics and my mother worked in the library. I was home for the intercession break, returned from California's Paradise Tech, where I was, precociously, doing my graduate studies. A drunk left over from Christmas was careening down the left side of Route 61, in Olympia, New York, a bare fifteen minutes after the music faculty of Olympia College had completed its performance of Schubert's *Unfinished* (or so have I, perhaps too symbolically, remembered it), which no doubt Cynthia and Jake Childs had applauded until their soft white palms had gone to tingling red. Amateur musicians themselves, they never stinted on ovation.

I can summon my mother exactly as I, sitting cross-legged

on my boyhood bed, last saw her: girlishly ablush to be going out with her Jake, struggling into her bulky red-and-black-checkerboard woolen coat, which my father, over six feet tall, held too high for her, who stood barely five, and whose glance of startled gratitude at his habitual gallantries remained firmly fixed even when her glasses were, as a direct result, sent flying from her nose. He was her gallant hero, brilliant, Anglo-Irish, and tall, who had rescued her from the state of being Cynthia Rosenthal, a homely girl who sat alone and read and stared at stars and read and sat alone.

I had not accompanied my parents to their concert that evening because, unlike them, I dislike music. To my senses, it is a deliberate din, perversely prolonged. I read once that the music of Mozart is to be compared with the play of light on water. I know something of the physics of the play of light on water and can make no sense of the analogy.

My two parents, the suddenly entragicked Cynthia and Jake, were both lovers of music in its many varieties. Music constituted the one small point of nonconvergence between my parents and me, and from it proceeded a nonconvergence elongated through all eternity.

The light went out. There was no light, there was no logic. How could it be? It was years before I knew, but then I knew.

We each carry our own designated end within us, our very own death ripening at its own rate inside of us. There are insignificant people who are harboring unawares the grandeur of large deaths. We carry it in us like a darkening fruit. It opens and spills out. That is death.

The drunk died too. Had he lived, I suppose I would have learned earlier the qualities of hatred that I now know.

Because I was an only child I was never given the opportunity to hate a sibling. I never wanted one, of course, girl or boy, the difference wouldn't have mattered. I don't think that

I ever formulated a conscious desire that no other child appear to wrest from me my exclusivity. The possibility was so unthinkable that it simply never crossed my mind. We composed a perfect solid: pyramidical, self-contained, complete.

She was an only child, too. We were alike in that. And now she is an orphan in the world, quite almost alone as I, the cruel edge in the cold quite almost as permanently fixed, in this town whose name I can't recall, even though it is a name that a young man might wear on his chest like a ribbon, or at least once could, before the young ladies arrived.

Yes, the young ladies now occupy the campus. They sleep in sweatpants in hard and narrow dormitory beds. They take notes in the great lecture halls, where the voices of long-gone professors still echo at these odd hours, mingling true beliefs with false. The women's lacrosse team is a coven of champions.

It was very different when I first came here. The young ladies used to arrive at the briefly unmonked campus only for weekends then, when football games were played or special social occasions declared. The . . . weekend. The . . .

Have I forgotten or did I never know?

And the name of the Fluff-and-nut sandwich.

I would see the young men waiting at the little train station, stamping their feet to stay warm in the winter, the steam rising from their open mouths and flaring nostrils, the long scarves in the dyadic colors of the school wrapped around necks ranging from scrawny to brawny. The nondescript room I rented was not far from the little station. On Friday afternoons, I would often be there to watch the gilded girls alight from the rinky-dink train that connected the town's stop to the main line.

I remember all the girls who stepped off that train as beautiful. Even when bundled up for winter, they were more akin to shimmering orbs of radiance than the more lumpen manifestations of matter who awaited them and who were unspeakably unworthy.

Not that I deemed myself worthy. Or did I? No, I did not. The sight of beauty is naturally intimidating, imposing silence on our quibbling nature. And yet I had discovered, only shortly before my arrival here, the startling fact that I myself was good-looking. I still didn't know what to do with the fact. I believe I never did figure it out. It was a fact that remained only haphazardly attached to my sense of me, that dangled awkwardly. It had been pointed out to me, my second year as a graduate student, by an admirer of the altogether erroneous gender, but it was authentic information nonetheless. I saw that it was true and was amazed. Only someone who had so justifiably earned the hurled epithets — *nerd! geek!* — could have missed detecting the fact for himself. My father's androgynous symmetry of feature, his taut and pale complexion, conjoined with the eyes and hair of my mother, hair dark and crêpey and eyes speaking extravagantly of soul, had produced in me this dangling situation.

I knew enough — I was not an idiot — to know that the fact of my being actually good-looking (I think, perhaps, very) had an intimate connection to the state for which I longed: my addressing, in so many words (which?) one of the alighting young radiants, her meeting my gaze and . . . so on . . . and on . . . in ways I barely dared to distinguish in any consecutive order. I only reveled in the shining obscurity of their ongoing. I had never known such girls as those, not to speak to, to touch with the fingers of my hands.

My watching was of a quality distinct, I think, to me. I felt the light of those girls drawing out my own, fingers of light originating in my brain and stretching out from my eyes in a trembling agony toward them, to almost touch, to glance off them lightly. I had felt those luminous digits as a boy, piercing my telescope's lens to probe the dim, dark bodies splayed gently on the wide night sky. Some girls sensed my mystic fingers on them, or so it seemed. Perhaps many more than betrayed in outward signs the sudden flare of gnosis: the shuddering knowledge of emergence, to know and to be known. Keeping apace with the banality at her side, a disappearing fairy girl would cast a quick glance back. I waited for the one who would turn to me and stay, an answering angel.

— *Who are you?*
— *Dana Mallach.*
— *His daughter, then.*
— *Yes, his daughter, yes.*

Now, in this ravishing season, am I become once again a seasoned watcher, returned to this town that encloses my hate. I would follow her anywhere. Through hollow lands and hilly lands. I would find out where she has gone.

I am here.

I pause for a few moments at the end of the block to collect myself. To collect and recollect the essence that is me.

I am a real thing and really exist.

When I came here the first time I had not known yet that she existed. It is a fact: there once had been a time when I did not know her, did not love her and did not hate her. I barely knew then that he existed, her father, who was Samuel Mallach, and who was, like me, a physicist, but of even more than singular promise.

He had published an extraordinary paper on quantum mechanics, his paper of 19 . . . . Its year escapes me, though its content had once reconfigured all the world for me.

The knowledge of the physics trickles back, little though

I care, I find that it comes back, how stunned I'd been by Mallach's work, the introduction of the so-called hidden variables that had reattached the dangling formalisms of that grotesque theory to a world recognizably our own. His was a feat that had been deemed to be impossible by nearly all who were given to thinking on these matters. Physicists were in a mood to abandon reality to stuff more spectral than material, to the discrete events of observations and measurements, with nonexistence leering obscenely in between.

I had been outraged on behalf of reality, and so, for many decades longer, had Samuel Mallach.

It comes back to me, the cooled-off memory of all my white-hot fervor, the physics that had burned its way through the hours of my nights and days, the hours of my life. Mallach's hidden variables restored the objectivity of matter, which is to say that they restored matter. Mallach's paper de-loonied the electron, and put the psychosis back in the psyche, where it belonged.

Samuel Mallach was a great physicist, but with a wound to the soul that proved eventually fatal. His death, the second one, the one more final, was not, in the end, my fault. This I can recall with absolute authority: that I am no murderer. She and her father were wrong to paint me so, to cast me in the form of monstrousness, withdrawing all possibility of pity.

A Fluffernutter! That was the name of my most favorite sandwich, and it was no foreign word at all. There is a treachery in the seeming certitude of memory, and I must accept as a rule for the direction of mind that recollection is as suspect as a discovered liar, hiding a secret shiftiness inside. *Pfeffernuss* is no thing at all, a nothing in the world at all, but a phantasm tossed up out of lawless associations of the mind, of ideas colliding as in the very jumble of the mad, who also rave and reify, though they are mad, and I am not, in all probability I'm not, the mad almost never pose the question of themselves.

He had done the impossible, had displayed the electrons moving in coherent pathways. *Electrons are there,* one could say against the cult of scientific obscurantism. *Electrons move.* But because what he had done was considered by his colleagues to be impossible, the work had gone unseen. The impossible has a way of passing unnoticed among us.

He wandered the hallways of the department like a ghost and was condemned, for his quantum heresy, to teach the course they called "Physics for Poets." But he had taken to his sentence with an unbecoming gladness. It was the first work since the hidden variables that he had loved, although he was far more taken with the poets than the physics. He was teaching Physics for Poets to the baffled undergraduates who had wanted only to fulfill their science requirement without being dragged through the mental anguish that they called mathematics. The tag was meant to convey only what was mercifully missing, but he had taken fiercely to the notion of the noetic poetic.

The undergraduates were, to say the least, underwhelmed. He stood before them and sang songs of Blake. The students complained in droves, even though problem sets were seldom, and the grades, albeit random, were high-ended. Some in his class were sufficiently vexed to transfer to real courses and take the consequences.

He set me to study lines of words of his own choosing. He gave me the Willies, William Blake and William Yeats, poets of glimmer and gloom. That was how he thought to prepare me for the formidable problem that we were once hell-bent on solving, and that would, had we but solved it . . . had we but only solved it . . .

I am Justin Childs, and am something so long as I believe

that I am something and am Justin Childs, a thing that hates.

The houses, well placed on their tender spreads of lawn, are all in darkness at this hour. There are ancient trees and expensive shrubs sealed up in smug shadow. The trees, coated on top with the thin milk of the moon, shiver slightly.

A heavy limb cringes with a drawn-out groan, and the low leaves mutter with the prejudices of matter.

How full of false opinions the vegetative souls are.

The sign that stands at the end of the block is lit by moon and gives its name. This is Bagatelle Road. Each home on it aspires to another place, another time, aspirations very characteristic of these surroundings. There is not what I would call an American house on the entire length of Bagatelle Road, nothing like the American house of my perfect-solid boyhood.

From my place beside the moonlit signpost, I can only just make out her house. The disturbances in the field disturb the patterns of my seeing. There is a field of forces radiating outward from that house, and this field is highly charged for me, uncohering my history.

What thing am I? What thing?

The lines of force hum louder, a humming like that of electrons surging through hot wire, a mosquito in one's ear whose hum is madness.

Every instant now is a lifetime full of passions and perturbations, intermingled with the scents of the past, so that the breath of her shampoo, which had once pierced me through and through, now pierces me again. I did not gasp aloud, I do not think, I do not gasp aloud, only one must take them all more slowly or be whelmed over, move less eagerly than one would wish.

Eagerness, above all else, must be resisted. Eagerness would be the end of me. What is required is a detachment perfectly cold. What is required is to move and not be moved. Nothing shall move me.

I am Justin Childs, and the essential fact is that I hate her.

It is an English Tudor, very elegant and self-contained. It, too, appears to be given over to darkness, like its night-musing neighbors, but I know better. This is not, by any means, my first night visit, and I know that even when she does manage her few fitful hours of sleep, lamps are always left burning, testament to her uneasy soul.

She is frightened of darkness, but she dreams, I think, of fire. I see fire in her dreams.

Quite often I find her up, wandering her big and empty house in the small hours, leaving lights on wherever she goes.

And I am here, and I know by that humming, whose noise is like madness, that she is near, within this house, and that, afraid of the night, she waits it out, awake.

It is a beautiful house. Its dimensions, too, once diminished me, passed over me like a felt eraser and left me smudged, but now I am changed and less subject to erasure. The house had once belonged to her maternal grandparents. It was her mother, the long-gone Dotty, I at least called her Dotty, whom I had learned adroitly to despise, who had brought the wealth into the family, the evidence of which had served to deepen the disorder of my state on my first visit here. It becomes a physicist to be a materialist only in the most abstract of senses, asserting that all is matter, that the properties of matter in motion are the properties that there are. What business had a theoretical physicist with so much wealth? And Samuel Mallach was a most unworldly man, an otherworldling who wandered the hallways of his department unnoticed, a man with no sense of intellectual fashion, a defeatist slope to his person, and the odor of the old insanity still wafting faintly about him. Each madness has an odor of its own, and most of them are nasty.

She has finished her schooling. She is now formally, officially, schooled. She has as many degrees as I. But she has come home, and interred the diplomas in some unvisited bottom drawer. She is an heiress, having come into legacies of more than one sort, of money and memory and more. She lives alone in the beautiful home where she grew up, in this town that comports itself with a dignity so perfected it has almost the marmoreal aspect of death.

It is strange of her to have returned. Did she think the deviance in my coordinates would carry me away, cancel my essence and nullify my hate?

I am *her* hidden variable.

Around to the back, where the opaque architecture gives way to glass.

It was one of Dotty's last projects, to break her house open to transparency, so that there is a dazzling eruption of unloosed light, of photons streaming reckless into night, summoning from out of the nearby woods the hosts of fragile creatures, beating furious wings in light-fed frenzy, while others, immobilized by love, are flattened on the glass as if painted there, wings outspread, a breathless attending upon the blaze from within.

Dressed in a long white robe, and she is wintry pale in high summer, and we are separated only by the frozen breath of this thinnest glass. She sits immersing a straw tea basket into a porcelain cup, slowly dipping down and up, a meditation on the infusion of green tea.

She is beautiful still, while I am so ruined, although she, too, has been retouched by calamity. A few odd years have passed, some three or five or seven, and still her hands and arms are marked by the discolorations that were left behind, the ghosts of flames still reaching toward her shoulders, and beneath the robe there is a leg that must limp, and the memory of fire still burns loudly in her dreams. I do not see her dreams, but still I know, and I have watched her eyelids shiver frightened over visions.

Held captive on the glass, wings outstretched and unmoving, the light-headed moths and light-headed me, pressed flat against the smooth, hard surface, while she, the object of our stares, gazes down into her steaming tea, the lovely lovely lovely of her face still partially, mercifully, veiled, while I am ruined.

I am Justin Childs and am something so long as I think I am something, let him who would deceive me try his best, I am and am and am

Damned.

I must strengthen myself before those eyes, their held hue and life and light and sight, her slender hands wrapped round the pale green cup, whose contents go untasted, for her musing mood is on her.

I know the mood but not the musings. Her musings are her own. She has an inner life, that is the sorry truth. They mostly do, to some extent, but she takes it to the extreme. There is a universe in there, a curved and closed infinity. So beautiful a form: why could it not have been the all? The image in the mirror, why could it not have been the all and all?

> *The love-tales wrought with silken thread*
> *By dreaming ladies upon cloth*
> *That has made fat the murderous moth.*

Read Yeats, her father had instructed me. Read Blake. Having lost his physics, together with his senses, to the devastations of vast sorrow, he was desperately seeking it in poetry.

He's mad, I thought, but I'll still get the physics from him. I'll get the glorious physics out from him.

She has stolen it from me. She took from me the ancient dream of fire and divinity, to plunge into the fire and emerge a god. She has stolen it from me.

Behind the glass, she dips her tea and doesn't see the silent congregation gathering. The glass is thick with watchers.

I am a real thing, and really exist; but what thing? I have answered: I have answered.

Sometimes she reads and sometimes writes. I have seen no mathematics in her writings, but that proves nothing. Her imagination, like her father's, travels other paths.

Dawn will be here soon. Wearily she'll climb the stairs, leaving the lamps still lit below, to burn away into invisibility in the daylight.

Motionless we watch, the famished moths and famished I, pressed up against the glass, while behind us, there is an erupted madness of movement, a dry fluttering as if of émigrés from Hades, starers starving for the light, driven past their limits by the properties of radiance, their need pressing like the weight of mortality within, so that occasionally, as now, there is one so sent by desire that it dies against the glass, with the sound of something fragile breaking.

It is a shatter barely sensible against the treachery of things too transparent, the soft sound of some too soft creature dying softly for the light.

Even so, it is heard within.

She starts and looks up quickly, the gnosis of green tea forgotten, the hot liquid spilling over trembling hands, and the violence of the shudder pulling all her features along with it, so that she is, for the moment, an ugly woman, an unchosen girl cast out of the golden net.

In her eyes there is an articulation of terror so stark it

seems that of a very small child. Or something drawn by a child.

It makes one smile to see a child's hand scrawl across the features of that face, unforming their beauty.

A sight to behold, she stares back at the starers thickly clustered on her glass . . . one of whom is smiling.

She believes in ghosts. Poor child, she believes in me.

II

"Do we believe in souls, Justin?"

The large bay window of her bedroom was flung wide open, and through the filmy curtains drifted the fragrant urgings of the summer night.

Slowly, they had come apart from each other. He had watched their bodies separating as she had lifted herself away from him, her face turned to the side so that he was unable to read the shape of its expression.

They both had bodies that were narrow and very white; though the summer was well advanced, mid-August, they were both winter-pale, their days spent deep down in their enclosed pyramid with the wild properties of light.

She lay back, her hair slightly damp and darkened against the white pillow. When she was lying down like this, there was a hollow high up on each leg that he thought must be unique to her, heartachingly formed. He thought it would be impossible for him ever to love a woman who lacked this precise ellipse carved into each thigh. Her stomach, too, was concave and lovely, so much loveliness, and the moaning fragrance of the summer night pouring into the room.

There was only the thin light of the moon, and he needed to see her more clearly, to see how the momentary expression of her face was set. He switched on the little lamp beside her bed.

"Too bright, it hurts," she said, and, leaning over him, she fished out a black silk scarf from her night-table drawer and flung it over the light. She turned back to him then as she had been before, one arm cast back over her head, slightly altering the shape of her breasts, and she repeated her question.

"We believe in bodies, Justin, but do we believe in souls?"

Only minutes ago, sitting astride him, she had seemed almost terrifying in what she knew. Now he could see her in the silk-darkened light, her pupils large and almost entirely blotting out the blue, and he saw that she was smiling, her lips playfully curved, although she wanted him to answer. He could read the intent out of her mouth. Sometimes she was like this, childish and charming, and other times she terrified him by what she knew.

"Of course not, Dana. We're scientists, physicists. How can we believe in souls?"

Her lips were slightly bruised, swollen from his hard kisses. At first she hadn't wanted to kiss, it seemed to be the only thing their bodies could do to each other that made her uncomfortable. Now she hardly ever resisted his mouth against hers. Sometimes, though this was rare, he even found her mouth initiating the search after his.

"I can. I'm fully capable of believing myself possessed of an immortal soul. I think I'm even capable of believing you possessed of something vaguely soul-like."

The wounded lips made her seem even more like a child to him, as if she might have hurt herself by falling from her bike or tumbling out of a tree, and it stirred up tenderness, too much coming too quickly. He felt the frightening rush of it and let it escape in something like a laugh.

She smiled back, childish and charming.

There was little of the terrifying girl to be seen in her now. Only minutes before, she had moved over him so knowingly, all his desires in her tight grip as if she inhabited his mind, had access to the sensations of his body, knew his desires far better than he. Now she gazed at him like a child, waiting for him to answer.

"I meant justifiably, Dana: How can we believe in them justifiably?"

"Oh, justi*fi*ably!"

She was grinning broadly with her poor abused lips. He leaned over on his left elbow and kissed her. She turned her head away.

"Are they sore, your lips?" he asked, running a finger lightly over them.

"Mmm, now that you mention it. Brute."

"Soulless brute."

"All brutes are soulless. Therein lies the difference."

"All things are soulless, including you."

"Not me."

"Sometimes I think especially you."

She laughed, low down in her belly, so that he let his mouth move downward over her, his kisses tentative with doubt. He would never possess her certainty when it came to this sort of knowing. He still made mistakes, he made them often.

"Daddy believes just the opposite, you know."

Justin removed his mouth and looked up at her. Apparently, he had erred again.

"Daddy believes that all things are full of souls."

"Your father is a great physicist, Dana, not because he has such beliefs but despite them."

She smiled sweetly. It was an old argument between them, which was sometimes sweet and sometimes bitter.

Justin moved back up the bed so that he was lying beside her. He reached out again to run a finger over her lips, tracing them again and again, each time a little harder, and tried to imagine himself into her body. He had intimate knowledge of his doubts, while she always seemed to know how to make him feel exactly what she wanted him to feel.

Enchantress of the world.

She turned her head now to face him so that his finger slipped over her cheek.

"So you think it's just us and our bodies, then?"

"No 'and,' Dana. How can there be an 'and' when it's a single thing."

"I like the 'and.' I'm in favor of the 'and.' It seems too lonely without it."

"It seems lonelier to me with it. If you've got a soul concealed somewhere in here," he said, sweeping his hand from her shoulder to her thigh, his fingertips glancing the heartbreaking sweetness impressed in her flesh, "then how can I ever know it? How, Dana? I've got access to your mysterious body but not your mysterious soul. Souls seem to me the loneliest possibility of all."

"That's probably the best argument you can give for the soul's existence," she had answered him, laughing softly, with nothing of the child left there to be seen.

III

The moths are pressed up hard against the glass and they are famished.

Their bloodless bodies are easily crumbled into ash. They die against the glass and they are ash, and loneliness is the ether that they breathe. They breathe it in and breathe it out again, unaltered.

And souls are the loneliest possibility of all.

IV

He saw her the first time reflected in a mirror.

— I thought you weren't real.

— Not real?

— I thought you were a painting.

She was staring into a mirror that hung on the landing of the staircase of her house. He had been coming down those stairs, slowly groping his way down the length of their extravagance. Her image was in the mirror and across it light was spilling from a high window, so that he had been struck wide open to confusion, not having even known that she existed.

He had come here that day, to the beautiful house on Bagatelle Road, with a set purpose, to determine whether or not Samuel Mallach was a real thing, correlating to the author of the paper that had been his revelation. And if he were the Samuel Mallach whose hidden variables had accomplished the impossible, he meant to propose, with all the presumption of which he had once been so capable, a kind of collaboration.

It was an audacious plan, considering that he had completed his doctoral degree only the spring before. That had been accomplished in Paradise, California.

Paradise. He remembered that name. And he remembered that Paradise, California, had possessed hothouse beauties by the dozens, striding around with their tennis rackets swinging from their tanned arms, pedaling slowly by on bicycles. They wore pale pink and pale green and pale yellow, and their shining hair was kept from obscuring their bright visions of the world (for to what other visions might such girls be given?) with matching headbands.

The headbands most especially impressed and moved him, for they brought to mind vague notions of the invisible fingers of intentionality that had chosen these bright bits of ribbon, pointing to pathways of cerebration that were so mysteriously remote they might have been traveled by the Ra-worshipping Egyptians.

They made a different light in the Paradise day, those glinting girls, throwing it off as they drifted by. They made a light that struck an imbalance and wild awe wherever it hit, and awed, he thought it might have been that ancient light that was the sight streaming down from the sun god's one eye, although these were sun children of a different sort, of California, daughters of the Paradisian pharaohs, and even so, they were a revelation, in their canted beams and matching headbands.

Either there had not been girls quite like these back in Olympia, New York, or, living there with his two parents, in their perfect solid, he had simply failed to notice.

The girls of Paradise had been a revelation, but the physicists of Paradise had been something less. He had not liked what they said of matter. He had not liked what they said of the world. They had taken the difficulties in the fundamental theory of matter as a license to distort the nature of the real, so that Justin could not help but perceive their views as acts of ontological sabotage: maligning the objectivity of matter and unraveling the rationality of the world.

His sense of betrayal had been cosmic in those days, it had been something awful, the demon logic of the counterfactual chattering hideously through every waking hour of his days and nights.

He had such thoughts as these:

If only he, their only son, had accompanied them that December night, his indifference to their music might have hastened them along. Or perhaps it was rather that they had actually hurried away because Justin was waiting for them at home and alone. Poor Justin, one might have said to the other. Poor Justin, we've abandoned him on his first visit home. Either one of his parents might have said this, the other agreeing — *Justin abandoned!* — so that, had he but gone with them, they would have stayed the perhaps three or four minutes more that would have given them the rest of their lives.

In short, innumerable factors had conspired to bring about the initial conditions that had determined their deaths on Route 61 in Olympia, New York, and among them had been Justin's absence: a necessary though insufficient constituent of a causal antecedent that was sufficient though not necessary.

He had returned to Paradise Tech four days late after winter break. His roommate, Zeno Wicks, had told him that another day and he would have assumed that Justin was dead. This was most probably a joke on Zeno's part. In Justin's considered judgment, at that time and even later, it was a joke, and as such not really an appropriate invitation for a revelation on the order that was Justin's to give. So, quite logically, he said nothing, waiting for a better moment. He would tell Zeno or someone else, though most probably Zeno, when the moment was better, that he had used those four days to bury his parents. But for the next three and a half years that he and Zeno had lived together, there was never a moment better than that one that had come and gone. The further the event receded from the present moment, the more remote the chance of speaking of it became, though he dreamed of it, dreamed day and night, most especially that a fairy girl would turn to him and speak with the voice of an answering angel, and he would tell her and she would know.

Physics was all that remained from the time before. When Justin thought of physics, then the world seemed like the sort of place that he might know, a universe corresponding to the faculties of his own mind, the logos of his thought joined to the logos of the world. Therefore, Justin thought about physics, and earned a significant reputation, even in a place like Paradise Tech, though there was no one to care all that much when the time came that he was declared the best of his year, and then when the time came that he was declared much better than that.

But Justin had not liked what the Paradisians said about matter, he had not liked what they said of the world: the reckless spin they put on the physics of matter in motion. Olympia had not prepared him, the Olympians had confused his expectations.

There had been no question but that Justin would go to the local college, for he was only sixteen, had barely turned sixteen, when he graduated high school, and very young even for his age, too callow to venture out on his own, to live apart from Cynthia and Jake, none of them even considered it. He lived at home, ate almost every meal at home, a plate of deviled eggs to see him through the long nights of study. He was able to walk to the campus, a long steep climb up from the snuggled town to the modest college laid out sparkling on the hill.

He loved the walk best of all in the winter, through Olympia's endless show of snow. A cause for grumbling among many of the Olympians, for him it was intoxicating, the smell of snow in early morning. At night, in warmer months, after he had finished with his books, and his mother, dreamy-eyed behind the black-framed glasses, had washed and dried and put away the dinner things, the three of them, his father, too, or sometimes just the two of them, would go outside and lie on the untidied lawn, reticulating stars.

He had luxuriated in the palace of his mother's knowledge.

— *What do you study?*

— *Beauty.*

— *What shall I study?*

— *The same. In Greek, the word for the universe and for beauty are one: cosmos.*

He had been allowed to take his science and math courses at the college even while he was still in high school, his last two years in Ionia County High School, so it was a natural transition to go to Olympia College. It hardly felt like much of a change at all, only the classes got better, the teachers knew more, even though the emphasis at Olympia College had been on practical subjects like agriculture and engineering, and the three-man physics department justified its existence by teaching service courses to students from other departments. Justin had exhausted all the math and physics courses offered by the end of the first semester of his sophomore year, which might have left him up a creek without a paddle, as the chairman of the department, Professor Krebs, had put it.

"We've got to deliver you a paddle, son," said Josiah Krebs, who had no Ph.D., though he did have chickens, six or seven Rhode Island Reds, and a little daughter who looked like a fairy sprite and played her cello each year at the faculty Christmas party. The Rhode Island Reds laid eggs that were brown and very tasty, and he made gifts of them to his favorite faculty wives, among them the charmingly starry-eyed Cynthia Childs, who would devil them for Justin.

Professor Krebs devised a plan of independent study for Justin, and also arranged for him to be able to complete all of the requirements for graduation in three years, so that Justin went off to prestigious Paradise Tech when he had just barely turned nineteen, not altogether prepared for life among the non-Olympians, for the ways in which they slighted reality, for the ways in which they were stupid as only the really smart can be stupid, to subvert the objectivity of matter and unravel the rationality of the world. That was not the sort of thing he had ever once heard from affably agrarian, arguably absurd Professor Krebs, who had taught him quantum mechanics from Merzbacher's text with a certain show of suspicion.

— *It's so much cock-a-doodle-do!*

Yes, that surely qualifies as suspicion. He had a scrawny neck, Professor Cock-A-Doodle-Do, that he craned upward when he opined, showing the ovoid bulge of his Adam's apple. He was chairman of the Olympian physics department, but he was most proud of all of the powers of his laying hens and of his little girl. At four or five years old she was playing Mozart on a miniature cello.

"You can't really say what it's all about, now can you?" he had demanded of Justin, staring at Schrödinger's equation for the evolution of the wave function, symbolized by psi. Erwin Schrödinger, who had won his Nobel in 1933, had demonstrated that the wave function, a precisely defined mathematical object, completely specifies the state of any quantum mechanical system. So perhaps the most likely answer to Professor Krebs's querulously put question *What's it all about?* is that quantum mechanics is about the behavior of wave functions. But it had also been Schrödinger who had convincingly argued that because the wave function is stubbornly smeared out over configuration space, the abstract space of all possible configurations of the particles, until the precise moment of its collapse, it therefore resists all attempts to connect up with a world recognizably like our own. Faced with this intractability, formally known as the "measurement problem," many of the luminaries of physics, from Bohr and Heisenberg on down, took the radical step of denying the existence of an independently existing physical world altogether, and, surprisingly, got away with it. In other, i.e. nonscientific, contexts, the difference between those who are committed to an independently existing reality and those who are not is roughly correlated with the distinction between the sane and the psychotic.

"Stop admiring the pretty equations and answer my question," Professor Krebs had scolded. His tone of voice was of the sort to be correlated with a pursing mouth, but since his mouth was virtually lipless, it was difficult to tell. "You just can't say what it's all about, Justin Childs, I know you can't, because I've never heard anyone who could. Not so I've ever been able to understand it, anyway. It works just great as an instrument, it's a gimcrackery piece of machinery for manufacturing predictions. But so far as what it's saying about the world, at least so far as I can make it out, it's so much cock-a-doodle-do."

All the other graduate students at Paradise Tech had come from places far fancier than Olympia. Zeno had gone to the Micomicon Institute of Technology, and the difference between that school and Olympia became obvious to Justin pretty quickly. It was obvious that Zeno had never heard anything like Josiah Krebs declaring quantum mechanics so much cock-a-doodle-do. All during his first semester, Justin had felt like some sort of science hick, like a country cousin who couldn't tell spin up from spin down. It was only after he had returned from burying his two parents in the cemetery at the foot of the hill of Olympia College, almost directly situated on the other side from the steep road he used to climb in early morning to reach the campus, that he had come to realize the treachery of the slicks, elaborating the most convoluted theories in which to speak their nonsense, to say, for example, that *measurement creates reality, so that it is sim-*

ply meaningless to ask what's going on when no measurement is taking place.

Justin's father, too, had employed the strong potency of that word, "meaningless," but he had done so responsibly, turning it against only the fabrications of the metaphysicians and not against the world itself, not against the realities of matter, space, and time, and the laws of their causality.

In Paradise, Justin heard such notions as *the entire conception of an objective reality, existing though unobserved and unmeasured, has been invalidated by the discoveries of quantum mechanics,* so that Justin was enraged. He took the part of reality and was correspondingly incensed. All nonsense is an offense to truth, and this, fumed Justin, was nonsense so extravagant that it did not even succeed in being wrong. Men who ought to have known better had committed stupidity and offended reality, and Justin's outrage knew no bounds, could know no bounds. It was an outrage flowing outward, the vectors of attention turned away from the self and overflowing him altogether, his own personal rage blurring into the rage of a reality that had been slighted, that had been scorned, so that Justin Childs was spread out onto the real in a superposition of unappeasable wrath.

He had not liked what they said about matter. He had not liked what they said of the world.

There had been a great man who had produced an argument claiming to show the impossibility of any hidden variables to fill in the gaps in intelligibility and restore to matter its substance and independent reality — in short its materiality. The other great men had applauded and not bothered to look too closely for flaws. Physicists, in the name of some madness that had eluded him, were suddenly much taken with the idea that matter be irrational. Saul, en route to Damascus, had seen a vision and changed his name.

Pauli. Wolfgang Pauli.

Wolfgang Pauli had said that the quantum theory, complete as it was and wanting nothing more, had revealed the irrational in matter, and Bohr (of Copenhagen) and Heisenberg (of a very bad Berlin) had chattered in parallel lines that met, if not in infinity, in utter obscurity, and von Neumann signed in with a suspect proof, purporting to prove the impossibility of hidden variables.

Was it the baleful influence of the powerful mythologizer in Vienna, throwing the tangle of his myths over language and over mind? Physics must cope not only with the complexity of matter, but also its complexes?

Someday, when glaring Paradise, California, relentlessly sunny, was in the past, Justin planned to think more deeply on these matters, planned to see his way beyond the glare and into the clear. For the time being, his dissertation problem left him precious little time to think, but someday soon he would have the luxury of thinking on these more fundamental matters.

He had missed four days of classes, and had been forced, ever after, to work single-mindedly to make up for all the loss. No one ever missed classes at Paradise Tech. He was conscious of those four days for the rest of his years there, for the rest of his years.

Justin had, in accordance with the physics à la mode, to manipulate the formulas and give no thought to what they might mean. He had done this well, had arrived at some mathematically beautiful results, for his affinity with beauty was strong, because he came to beauty by way of his mother.

— *What do you study?*
— *Beauty.*
— *What shall I study?*
— *The same.*

His results had impressed the right heads, if for all the wrong reasons, and had secured him a post back east as a junior member at a most important place.

He might never have discovered Mallach's astonishments at all, if not, paradoxically, for his roommate. Zeno Wicks was studying solid-state physics, and had shown no appetite for bottom-feeding on questions of foundations. Zeno had, for the most part, been content to use quantum mechanics as they had all been taught and not to think about what it might actually be saying. However, Zeno's dissertation advisor was Nathan Martin, a Paradisian of the very top tier, not only a first-class researcher, but also reputed to be perhaps the most engaging lecturer in the entire world of physics, and Nathan Martin had a knowledgeable wife, at least for a short while, whom Zeno had met several times when he had visited their home. It had been Mrs. Martin who had mentioned the work of Mallach to Zeno, while her husband, asserting his conjugal rights, had vigorously scoffed. And though the scoffing had come from the very first tier, still Zeno had been moved by Mrs. Martin to seek out the Mallach paper for himself.

Even after Mrs. Nathan Martin was Mrs. Nathan Martin no more, the marriage packet suddenly collapsing and Nathan Martin remarrying with a speed concomitant with his power and reputation, still Zeno had tried to get through the paper. Justin had seen his roommate frowning over it now and again until finally letting it go, and it had gradually sunk lower in the debris lapping round their beds. A few weeks after Justin had completed his dissertation and been offered his prestigious post, he had rather idly fished it out and started to read.

Justin had read Mallach's paper with something like amazement, for in it he saw clearly that the impossible had been done: an objective model for quantum mechanics.

Mallach had formulated a hidden-variable version of quantum physics that had accomplished wonders for the material world, saved it from the mathemysticians, the kabbalists of Copenhagen, waving their hands and intoning their obfuscations, turning matter into a miserable ghost of itself, suspended in the not-quite-here-not-quite-there of quantum paradox, in which mess they reveled. Mallach's work, Mallachian mechanics as Justin would eventually dub it (though not without demurs from Mallach himself), was the very countercharm to break the vicious spell. (Mallach had not, in the least, objected to the adjectification of his name, but to the word "mechanics." "Call it better 'Mallachian nonmechanics,'" he had said, with his daughter, Dana, nodding approval.)

In Mallach's model, behind the vast thicket of thorny mathematics that spring up in these nethermost regions of physics, there awaited, like some fairy-tale princess, the electron, with real position and real momentum, everything real and existing even when unobserved, as well it should be, and it was this, that is the electron, that was the true value answering to "hidden variable." It was ironic that what should turn out to lie behind the mystery-mongering epithet of "hidden" was the most obvious choice of all, the electron, anointed now with existence.

Everything about Samuel Mallach's paper had been designed to astonish Justin, even the author's university affiliation, which was at the very place to which Justin was himself destined to go in less than six weeks' time. Or, in any case, Mallach had been present at the designated university when he had published his astonishing paper, which was, admittedly, already several decades old.

He must no longer be here, very possibly no longer alive, Justin had concluded after he himself had been teaching at the university for over a month and had heard no mention of Samuel Mallach's name, nor ever once caught a glimpse of him, not having realized that, on his very first day, Mallach had glided noiselessly past him in the department hallway. Justin had been standing there talking with his new chairman, Dietrich Spencer, an impatient man and high-energy physicist, who was, by common report, awaiting with high impatience the immortality distributed in Stockholm.

"Here, look — will you please? — while I explain the few formalities to you," Spencer had demanded of Justin, while at the same time snapping the fingers of his left hand three or four times at his side, a very characteristic gesture, though Justin, of course, had no way yet of knowing this, of knowing that the faculty meetings that Spencer chaired were almost continuously accompanied by this soft, insistent snapping.

It had startled Justin, this peremptory gesture of the fingers. He had thought that he must somehow have managed to anger Dietrich Spencer, and the dim alarm that the man had already set off in him was intensified to the point of sensible discomfort.

Dietrich Spencer seemed a physical energy that was barely compressed into a mass. His head was shaped like a bullet, just as hairless, and his neck and shoulders were powerful and broad. He was a contemporary of Mallach's, the two hired by the department in the very same year, a startling fact to contemplate, for Spencer certainly looked to be a man in the fullness of his prime, and if he wasn't, then it was slightly terrifying to imagine what the prime itself must have been like.

The most alarming feature of all was a long, thin scar that disfigured the left side of Spencer's head, crossing the high brow and ending right above his ear. Graduate students could be induced to believe that it had its origins in a duel, fought, so some embellished, in a suitably Gothic courtyard of Heidelberg. Justin always had difficulty keeping his eye from straying to its spot, that long thin scar, the skin of it unnaturally white.

Spencer had some sort of accent, impossible for Justin to place, though Heidelberg was often mentioned. His accent seemed to meander across the globe, in a voice that was strangely high-pitched for a man of his exaggerated physicality. His inadequate voice was an anomaly mildly reassuring, slightly neutralizing the effect of his compressed energy, the soft suggestion of violence embedded in his scar, in his methodical charm and subdued snapping.

Neither man, neither Spencer nor Mallach, had yielded recognition of the other, and the result had been that Justin, too, had barely noticed the wraithlike progress down the hall, swift and noiseless as it was. Like an electron's manifestation in a cloud chamber, a trail of vapor that appears and is gone, he barely seemed to register, and one was not altogether certain he'd been there at all. They were, in any case, Professor Spencer and Justin, absorbed in more immediate matters — Justin's teaching assignment, the daily teas that he was strongly urged to attend as frequently as possible — than the fugacious trail of a solitary physicist.

A few weeks later, Justin glimpsed the fact of Mallach. He heard someone call out the name, and he turned quickly to catch sight of the hastily receding figure just before it vanished.

Justin considered the possibility, although remote, of two Samuel Mallachs, both of them physicists.

One had published an astonishing paper some several decades before, which Justin had read and reread with something like amazement. The author of the paper had liberated matter from the jittery existence his colleagues had assigned it, of the flitting in and flitting out perhaps suitable for such things as memories and afterimages and . . . other dubieties, but not, let us grant, for matter.

And then there was this one, Mallach in the wearied flesh, who wandered the corridors of the department more ghostly than a ghost, avoiding everyone but the undergraduates, who largely avoided him.

He would not meet one's gaze. One could not bend that ray to meet one's own.

He was a burned-out star, they said (when they bothered to speak of him at all), although when he was little older than the twenty-three that Justin then was, Albert Einstein had confided in several colleagues that he regarded Samuel Mallach as his heir apparent. Now, in his black and cold contraction, Mallach instructed undergraduates, and even among these, the department's least favored.

The death of a star is a spectacular event, the most violent in all the cosmos, but Mallach seemed harmless enough (if one were not an undergraduate), mixing talk of photons with songs of Blake, bouncing back and forth between an anguished diffidence and intimations of awful transcendence.

Since physics is poetry, then poetry is physics, he propounded, with a lunatic's precision. And even so Justin had it in mind to get the truest strain of poetry from him. He and Justin: there was a complementarity there, although that was a word that Justin, on principle, eschewed, for it was a word that had been erected into a mystery religion for physicists. "Complementarity" was the shibboleth of the metaphysics mob, first assembled by Niels Bohr, founder of the "Copenhagen interpretation" and high priest of the quantum occult that had bedarkened the closing years of Einstein. "Complementarity" was the word by which the old Bohr breathed the viral germ of metaphysics into the sacred body of science and pockmarked suffering matter with hideous antinomies.

Metaphysics had broken out like a plague in physics' house. Mallach was, in his own way, as infected with the bug as the old Bohr, but his physics emerged nonetheless miraculously undiseased. He had some access more immediate. He felt the physics within himself, within the muscles of his own body. He told Justin this. He showed him. He danced for him once the movements of light in the two-slit experiment, the experiment that seems to lead paradoxically to the conclusion that light is like both wave and particle and that had been a spark igniting the conceptual explosion that became quantum physics. Mallach had danced away the paradox and Justin had not known whether to laugh or applaud, for the dance was absurd, and the dance was the truth.

Together, he and Justin, complementarily joined, might become the physicist necessary to perform the final reckoning; solve the formidable problem of merging the immiscibles of relativity and quantum truths; in short, show Mallachian mechanics to be Lorentz invariant, yes, and in the showing leap like mad Empedocles into the pouring fire and emerge . . . divine.

Justin, after all, possessed the mathematical pyrotechnics; this was acknowledged. This was the talent that had brought him, young as he was, to the attention of the luminous department. There were few physicists who could wield the fire of higher math better than he. Therein lay his singularity of mind.

But Mallach? There was no one, Justin knew this even if others did not, who possessed physical intuitions to compare with his. It was an uncanny process by which he invaded the *être intime* of matter. It was not mathematical at all, but some quite different form of imagination, more immediate than math. Perhaps he and Justin, together, might clear the remaining hurdle into the dazzle of that last problem's truth, like the ancient who had leaped into the lava.

So smoldering with expectation, Justin had approached the man as he went drifting by in the corridor not far from Spencer's office suite. The door to the outer office was open so that Spencer's thin voice, engorged now on anger, issued out into the hall. He was berating his two secretaries for their "mischief," a sardonic choice of word; it would be difficult to imagine two less mischievous sorts than Della and Joyce.

"Professor Mallach."

He had whirled around, startled into interaction, his face formally composed around a minimalist smile.

"Professor Mallach, I want to introduce myself to you, if I may. I'm Justin Childs."

"Are you one of my students, Mr. Childs?"

"I'm on the faculty here."

"Forgive me. I hadn't been informed. It is Professor Childs, then. Forgive me, forgive me." His voice was soft and halting, with a pronunciation as formal as his smile. "My rudeness was entirely unintended. And what is it that I can do for you, Professor Childs?"

Though he had looked taken aback when the unknown Childs had declared his wish to speak with him on physics, Mallach had quickly agreed to see him, in his home on Bagatelle Road, for he taught his classes and then fled the campus.

"Of course, I would be only too happy to discuss physics with you," though he frowned, and the look in his eyes declared that he was absolutely at a loss. "Come to my home, why don't you? I'm always at home, except when I teach my classes. And you will forgive me for not having known who you are, Professor Childs. I'm out of touch with the affairs of the department."

Mallach had met him at the door. Justin had rung the bell with its melodious ring, and the older physicist had answered the summons, gracious though bewildered, and then had led Justin up the grandeur of the swirling stairs to the small cluttered room that served as Mallach's study. He had books and papers, heaped one upon another. He was always searching through his random heaps, unable to lay his hand on the reference he knew to be there, somewhere concealed in the chaos, mumbling his bafflement aloud — *where, my God, where?* — though on the few occasions when his daughter tried to induce some order, he grew frantic and sent her away.

There was no other chair there but his own, so that when Mallach asked Justin, please, to take a seat, he had no choice but to remain upright, struck open to wide confusion.

The two of them were standing face-to-face amid the clutter of that study, a disorder that seemed to Justin to work, in some strange way, a process of detachment, removing the room from the interior of the house, which otherwise had the static stateliness of a museum.

A few minutes more of this face-off and Mallach went out to fetch another chair. It was an extremely large house, of whose total number of rooms, Justin, neither then nor ever, had a clear idea, and he quite justifiably wondered whether there might not possibly exist, in one of those ten or twenty or thirty others, two chairs on which two physicists might sit and discuss their science.

In any case, Mallach returned toting a large upholstered chair, which he squeezed inside the crowded space, and the two scientists were now well set up to discuss the nature of the universe, only they did not, so that all that Justin could do, struck open, was to wonder why Mallach had agreed to see him at all.

It seemed to Justin that Mallach was not acquainted with

his own work, that he was ill informed on what he had done, which had been, of course, the impossible. At every word Mallach spoke, his mumbly voice barely crossing the threshold of audibility, Justin was shocked anew. The little that was audible was shockingly askew.

Mallach had provided a model for what von Neumann and the others, who sneered at the "reality dogma," had said they had proved impossible. His hidden variables had broken the spell of subjectivity that physicists were trying to cast over the nature of matter, for in Mallach's model, the particles are real things and really exist, with determined positions and trajectories, their velocities expressed by the "guiding equation" in terms of the wave function, the entire configuration in this way evolving in a deterministic motion choreographed by the wave function, which is symbolized by psi.

The little that Mallach was mumbling seemed unintelligible. Justin listened to Mallach discussing the meaning of the wave function, and it was an elaborate lesson in the bizarre.

"I have been thinking recently that perhaps the wave function is more a verb than a noun. Then there would be no such thing as the wave function, and so no such problem as its collapse. The collapse of the wave function would be only a pseudoproblem made up out of syntactical errors."

Justin stared at the mumbling man in stunned dumbfoundment. He wondered: Is this some sort of test? Am I meant to cry out in the sacred name of sound reason and the existence of the material world?

"Perhaps alternatively," Mallach was saying in his faltering manner, "what we learn from the wave function is nothing of the system but only something of the systematizer, just as dream descriptions are only revelatory of the dreamer."

Each query that Justin sent out was lost in the foam Mallach churned up in its wake. Justin spoke, he thought, quite clearly, but Mallach gave him such baffled looks that Justin wondered if the man had lost his hearing and was not yet fluent at reading lips, so little did Justin's words affect the frothy progress, until Justin finally gleaned the truth, and it was this:

Mallach's work, having been declared impossible, had passed unnoticed among men, and now Mallach himself had entirely forgotten it. Justin could barely fathom how that could be, but it seemed that Mallach had lost the memory of his own physics. He had forgotten the illuminations of his own paper securing an objective model for quantum mechanics, barely remembered having published it at all.

"In your formulation, the collapse of the wave function comes about as a consequence strictly of Schrödinger's equation and your own guiding equation. There's no need for artificially invoking any special status for observation."

"I have been thinking that perhaps the Bard ought to be paraphrased to read: *We are such dreams as stuff is made of.* You see, Professor Childs, then we could assert that *stuff* comes from the *collapse* of the *dream.*"

Mallach removed his gaze suddenly from the window out of which he had been staring and looked directly at his visitor, so that Justin, for the first time, took in the physical presence of the man, took in the features of the ruined and handsome face: long and thin, the forehead furrowed and cheeks deeply creased; the nose also narrow and finely formed, except toward its end, where it took an extravagant dip downward toward the long, mournful line of the mouth. His eyebrows were unruly, unwinding coils of stark white hairs embedded in the black and gray, and beneath the anarchy of brows the dark eyes held the intrinsically sorrowful look that comes from being heavily hooded. It is a fact, probably of no

significance, that a disproportionate number of men of genuine genius have had such hooded eyes, and these two continued to gaze inquisitively into Justin's own, so that Justin
again considered whether he might possibly be the subject of
a subtly devised exam. Yes, perhaps it was an advanced form
of a test, after all.

"There's no place in your model for metaphors of dreams,"
he said with slow deliberation, carefully holding Mallach's
gaze. "There's stark lucidity, the electron's *there*. It's all too
lucid for metaphors and dreams."

Mallach had continued to stare at him, his smile still formally polite, though his foot had begun quietly to tap out a
rhythm of impatience.

"My guiding equation?"

"Yes."

"It is my guiding equation?"

"Yes."

"Do you mean $dQ \,/\, dt = (\hbar\,/\,m)\mathrm{Im}(\nabla\psi\,/\,\psi)$?"

"Yes. Why? Have you replaced that with some further
formulation?"

Mallach did not answer. From this point on, he said barely
another word.

The discussion appeared to do nothing so much as bore
him. Properties of matter and energy, of space and of time?
The intricate dance of waves and the particles of light?

He seemed impatiently indifferent. His long, thin legs, like
those of an improbably colored tropical bird, were crossed,
one over the other at the wasted knees, the right elbow was
poised on these, and atop the pile the head rested glumly in
the cupping right palm.

The supporting foot was tapping distractingly, a little more
loudly than before. He had the face of an ascetic after a long

penitential fast. His expression, as Justin spoke, suggested that his present visitor was yet one more penance.

He did not meet Justin's gaze again, but looked slightly aslant of him, sending his long sight back out the window.

What was the open book he had placed facedown on his desk? Justin tried to read the title, while also attempting to sketch for Mallach his own promising contributions to his ideas, the logical consequences he saw unfolding from the implicating order that Mallach had shaped.

Justin broached the formidable problem. If Mallach had no more thoughts left in him to give to the sweet possibilities of peer approbation, Justin would gladly make up the lack. What every genuine thinker — every genuine man, in fact — most craves is praise, though the thinker, with more delicate indirection, calls it "recognition."

Mallach was really no different, underneath it all, from anyone else. What, after all, had driven him so near the icy breath of madness (and was he not still mad?) but the enmassed indifference of his peers? Excluded by illogic, the cruel edge in the cold a permanent fixture.

He may be mad, Justin thought, but I'll still get the physics from him.

The head tinkerers, to whom Mallach had been forced to submit in his sadness gone berserk, had been, perhaps, a little too zealous in deracinating the madness, for they had uprooted the genius as well. Or perhaps it was the sadness itself that had sent the memory of his physics into hiding. He was so agreeably content to teach his Physics for Poets because he had some dark idea he'd find his answers there, that hidden away in some symbol-sodden sonnet was the something essential gone astray.

Only Justin, it seemed, still retained the memory of the

hidden-variable model, knew that it was possible, knew that it was true. Someone might have been tempted to take advantage of the situation.

Mallach barely heard Justin out that day. He did not even offer to see him down, a violation of the good manners that were all but involuntary to him. But his patience had been visibly worn away by the young man's fearsome tenacity. His foot had audibly tapped out his unrest, and the look in his eyes had declared he was at a loss. Had he said it aloud?

"I do not know what it is you want from me. I cannot fathom what it is you are after. Why don't you go and speak to my daughter? I have a daughter, you know."

Justin had not known.

Mallach's farewell had been hurried and included not a hint of an *au revoir*. Even before Justin had left the room, Mallach had taken up the book whose reading the visit had clearly interrupted. It was not even a book of physics. It was, as Justin finally saw, the poetry of Yeats.

> *The love-tales wrought with silken thread*
> *By dreaming ladies upon cloth*
> *That has made fat the murderous moth.*

Justin was disgusted. To the mind he then inhabited, a physicist who had forsaken physics was a prophet hiding his face from the one true God. Justin was (he is) an orphan. He knew (he knows) the orphaned state: excluded, forsaken, sick, sick for home, forever sick for a home that will never be again. Still, he did not yet grasp the nature of Mallachian despair.

In fact, Mallach then had seemed the most fortunate of men to Justin, to have accomplished a reconfiguring of reality around his hidden variables.

To reconfigure reality: it is the half of what makes a life decently significant. The other half is the praise of others. Why had Mallach, having secured the half, given up so soon, capitulated to the kabbalists of Copenhagen, turned away from configuring reality to stare instead at pretty words, at fluff of a nonmarshmallow variety?

The love-tales wrought with silken thread.

V

Lines of light and lines of longing, passing through me, unobservable, a thing that longs.

And nothing more? Am I nothing more?

I shall stop up my eyes, I shall call back my senses, I shall efface all the world from my thoughts, or, since this is barely possible, shall esteem it as empty and false, and thus holding converse only with my own self, and studying my own nature, shall endeavor to attain by degrees a greater familiarity and intimacy with the thing that I am.

I am a thing that remembers.

I saw her face the first time in its reflection. She was staring into this mirror.

I had not known before that moment that she existed. I did not know it even while I saw. It was her father I was searching for, not yet knowing of the daughter's existence.

The mother had died, an alcoholic death, it appears to be a theme.

Dana was very devoted to her suffering father, attending to him, whether in his melancholy brooding or fleeting fits of inspiration, in the town whose name I cannot recall.

The stars are threshed, and the souls are threshed from their husks. This I recall. It is Blake.

The earth has tilted and the night now is very long. It is the season of diminished daylight, diminished desires, and still I am here. Blind motion rules the world, and the world is full of tilt.

When I came that day it was in autumn, and I passed through the door and up these curling stairs, like the shimmery inside of a shell, a passage from a dream.

A prince might climb these stairs to find his pleasure.

So let me find my pleasure.

It is time, after all, that makes the difference. Remark the difference that separates time's deep and steady stillness from the thin drip-drip-drip of the now. It is the universe's very best trick. Figure it out and you've figured out a beauty, recherche'd your way to temps perdu, to the dark bright mystery on the other side of light.

I followed wordlessly after him, my mind on the possibilities of our collaboration, mounted these swirling steps as now I cannot, assaulted here by moments here and moments gone, the drip-drip-drip of now, momentarily battered by the shallow trickling of time, laced with terrors of longing, on stairs that lead to regions one can barely contemplate, as distant as pity, infinitely remote and steps away: the long dark corridor of unglimpsed links.

I had thought to propose to him that he and I might work together, together approach the formidable problem of merging quantum reality, now clarified through his work, with Einstein's truth. He had presented a realistic model of non-relativistic quantum mechanics. The task now was to reconcile it with relativistic time.

The passage of time is nothing real but a projection from our inner worlds. We know this from Einstein's physics, which shows us a time as stilled as spread space. Time is static, the flow unreal: it is Einstein's truth, and it is the truth. The flow of moments, which seems so relentless and so real, which seems to carry off one's every treasure, leaving one like a chest spilled open on the waves: unreal, unreal. The enigma is that a seeming correlate of that unreal time is present in the quantum world, tangled in quantum entanglement itself. I meant to make that problem mine and with it make my life.

It was her image that I saw first, as she stared into this mirror. I was about to descend, my foot was in midair, seeking the solid state of stair. It was late afternoon, and there was a shaft of autumnal sunlight from the skylight above that left her in the shadows like cobwebs clinging while it fell across her mirrored image.

A trick of the light; I know something of these. I had published several promising papers on the problems of partial diffusion. I saw her face in its reflection and, beset by partial confusion, first thought it a portrait, framed in gilt, capturing a moment in the life of a young girl who wore an expression of the utmost strangeness on her otherwise hopelessly lovely . . . lovely . . .

Lovely.

How to describe that face that had been startled into staring wonder, a girl hammered out of furious gold: I cannot. I see it now before me, but cannot. Yes, her hair was light, yes, I can say that, and that her eyes were blue, because I know it and see it still, the Irish blue, Hibernian blue, in hue Hibernian blue, but in their secretive veil, speaking of extravagances of soul, the other strain, the father's line, the duality of her lines of descent the mirror image of my own, and they were carried through into her *lovely, lovely, lovely,* as the hosts cried one unto the other, and said *holy, holy, holy,* though properties of matter all, but what were those properties that made that face that face, oh God that face?

I lose my drift and am in danger of losing far more, for it might possibly be the case that if I ceased entirely to hate *that I should likewise cease altogether to exist.*

I had thought it was a painting hung upon a wall and framed in gilt. So still, she stared, a soundless gasp formed by her features of wild wonder.

It was a look that I had dreamed to startle in a face, to startle deeper down inside. Alighting from the train, one would turn back to me and gaze, astonished into knowing. But I mistook the seized expression before me as merely representational, hung soulless behind clear glass, and no fingers of light had gone forth to tremble out its secrets.

Later and later, after days and even weeks of reliving her

face, I realized why it was that she was gazing in the mirror with that look of violation.

It was, of course, because she had caught *my* reflection in this gilt-framed glass, the staring stranger poised in the disequilibrium of interrupted descent. The simplest of optical laws: light travels in straight lines. If I saw her image, then she saw mine.

When she whirled around to face me, it was with still that wildness of stare. The one I returned her must have been just as sick with startle.

— *I thought you weren't real.*

— *Not real?*

Her voice was a hoarse whisper, and nothing lilting, as if it were being forced out of lungs that were ruined. She shook her head, to indicate a loss for something more in the way of speech. I answered her in kind. Like mirror images, we reciprocally shook.

— *I thought you were a painting.*

Her eyes were a blue, both cold and searing, I'd never seen, and I was, with all the certitude of well-formed instinct, afraid.

— *Who are you?*

— *Dana Mallach.*

— *His daughter, then.*

— *Yes, his daughter, yes.*

Her image was contained in here, this sheet of deadened glass that gives me nothing back, her eyes opening wide in startled attention at the intruder breaking and entering into her self-reflection.

She had been staring into this glass, and why, I wonder. In the moment before I came upon her she might have been arranging her hair or losing herself in the metaphysics of self:

Who am I, and what, and where, and whatever it is that I

am, how can it be that I am it, just this one and not another, that I am some something in the world, and not the world itself or something like it?

I don't think I ever again saw her glance into a mirror.

The lines of light pass coldly through me, they pass me by, I am a thing hideously unmirrored, the glass empty like the vacant eye that the pitiless show, or like, yes, far more like and awful and true, a young man's eye subjected to a violence of unvisioning, a mirror of the world no more, and there is a girl who squats in the grass beside him, the meaningless message of her chattering teeth the only comment offered in the suddenly split night, so great a silence after so great a noise, and that dead eye filling up with blankness, like this emptied eye before me.

I once had thought that darkness was the something real and light was bare privation. Darkness had seemed to me to carry the heft of substance, enough to hold the weight of predication. I had thought it was the properties of darkness that splashed colors over the world.

We had lain beneath the tree in our backyard, in the mythical land of distant Olympia, with a flashlight playing over the underside of the inky leaves. The man beside me was my father. No metaphysician would have been safe in his presence, but I was safe. Even in the dark, dark night, safe as safe could be. He had little patience for propositional nonsense, but he was infinitely patient with me.

— *Look, Justin. See the light up there in the tree. Where did the light go?*

My father flicked the instrument so that the end of it was now facing out into the darkness and there was no more light.

— *You turned it off.*

— No, I didn't, look.

He took my little hand and laid it over the flashlight's end and my hand's darkness melted away. There were my fingers: one, two, three, four, five. He flicked the torch back against the bark of the trunk, and I followed the spectral orb as it traveled up the trunk, up into the rustling treetop and then out into midair, where it was swallowed and seen no more.

— Me!

My father handed the flashlight over into my own small hands, so small that the heavy flashlight needed them both to hold it aloft, and I pointed the beam up into the leaves, and felt the fingers of light reaching out and up to touch the leaves that spread themselves above us. I rubbed the darkness off, and where I rubbed dim colors came, but the instant my fingers of light left the surface of the leaves, the darkness spilled back over.

I have ascended. The stairway swirls away beneath me.

Mallach led me up into this room, his cluttered study, that autumn afternoon, and we sat across from each other. I had waylaid him as he tried to drift invisibly past me in the department hallway, and he had bade me come to his house to talk about physics, but why he had so bade me I could only wonder now. He was eminently polite, although his crossed leg jiggled with impatience and his expression was bemused, as if he could make no sense of what it was I was saying, as I could make no sense of him, each of us dumbfounded by the matted meaninglessness of the other. He had books and papers, physics, metaphysics, theology and poetry, heaped one upon another, cohabiting and crossbreeding in this room as they did in his violated mind.

Now it is tidied up, this room, the labor of my Dana, who lives only to sort it out, by the dark lights of her despair. She thinks to lead a useful life through this, she thinks to be redeemed. She thinks to think of nothing else, but perhaps she will think again.

There is old sorrow heaped up high here in the corners, the stale odor of her father's old despair, desolating his senses through all the years since she had died, the giddy woman whom he had seen fit to call *extraordinary*. Her exit, drunk against a township tree, had worked to loosen his ontic attachment, that and his world failure. Attachment had gone slack in a way that wouldn't retract, each tug and it hung looser, and Dotty's death was such a tug, a hefty one.

There is a conclusion to be drawn from that. Disagreeable deduction.

The sickness of his old sorrow still hangs thick. Each madness has an odor of its own and I know his, as I know hers, for the smell of her madness is in this house, too, Dana's own madness, from which I had thought, madly, to save her.

One sees how it was, that I loved her. Another deduction. Will inference never cease?

I am a real thing and really exist, but what thing, what thing, I am what thing?

The haunted child would walk this unlit corridor, its length made double and triple by her frantic vision. I see her now approaching from the far end, her groping eyes sifting through the darkness, grain by grain.

— *Every night, Dana?*

— *Mmm. Until one night my mother woke up and saw me standing at her doorway. She got me to tell her what I was doing and how I did the same thing every single night. That I would see things, terrible things, and that I'd come to check that she and Daddy were all right. She told my pediatrician, and he prescribed some sort of pediatric tranquilizer. I was sedated from age eight to eleven.*

She spoke like the little girl that she had been and still became sometimes, childish and charming, the girl who lacked
the terrifying knowledge, and I teased her that the early se-
dation was the explanation for why she had never grown to
her full height, for judging by her long, tapering fingers, she
ought to have been a taller woman than she is. It was either
the lack of sleep or its brutal cure, I teased her, that had kept
her from attaining the full stature for which she had been
intended.

She is slowly coming toward me, the little barefoot girl in
the long white nightgown, the drip-drip-drip of time disor-
dered, so that I can see her approaching down this long unlit
corridor. As she would nightly go, so she goes now, on her
way to her parents' room, and she will soundlessly open the
door and watch them sleeping side by side in their shared
bed. I could trail her as she goes and see them for myself.

She approaches and will pass me by, padding softly on small
icy feet, and I can see how the properties of darkness have
swollen her pupils so that her eyes are given over to black-
ness, how they peer for the intruder in her house, and she is
coming toward me, and passes so near that I can feel the pitiful tremble that the life makes within her and I am here.

I am awash, I am awash, for it is Dana's room, Dana's room,
Justin Childs is in Dana's room, and I am Justin Childs.

And how singular is my position, what a singularity it is
that I inhabit, so that she ought to pity me, why can't she
pity me? I'd pity her to know her so, I'd pity her to the deepest regions where pity can go and I'd cry out for pity's sake —
for pity's sake — that I could go no farther, that I could not go
with her through all those endless reaches one is made to
wander alone, so far a distance from pity's touch and pity's
voice.

It is Dana's bed, it is Dana's bed, and the smell that is of her comes into me like my own deepest thought, only deeper than thought, and I must still myself, move less eagerly than I would wish, eagerness now would be the end of me, eagerness above all else must be resisted. I must force my way back into immobility, press myself back and yet farther back until I am contained in absolute stillness.

I would not move a muscle, so long as she slept, and I watched her eyelids shiver over her dreams.

— *Do you dream of me, Dana?*

I am no dream, though I may haunt her sleeping dawns as I haunt her sleepless nights, I am no dream.

It is her bed, it is her bed, and it must take me in now, as once it did, even as I am now, it is her bed.

It was a different Dana in this bed, that is a part of it, of the ache that opens wide to fill with ecstasy and empty out again, a different Dana suddenly revealed, that is a small part of it, of the awful mysteries held in the body motions of love, to watch in wonder that someone other who steps out, the secret other never seen by unchosen eyes. You see it emerge, and the sight of it is such a startling sweetness to the soul, the sight and the touch of it. With the fingers of my hands she led me to the hidden otherness of her.

It was a different Dana here, where now there is no Dana, no Dana sleeping here, with eyelids shivering over frightened dreams. Dana's bed is stripped, the house around it icy cold, with panicked molecules of air seeking their escape. Her bookshelves are bare, and her closets emptied out. She has taken her books and clothes and fled this town whose name I think now I shall never recall. She has fled and taken all my world from me.

It was a different Dana in this bed, a different Dana suddenly emerging. I do not think I gasped aloud, not aloud, I do not think, but I could not stop the trembling, to behold her swift emergence from the other, a different Dana revealed in the body motions of love.

I had come for dinner. We all drank wine, there were expensive bottles stored up still in the cellar from the days of drunken Dotty. We had begun our work together, Mallach and I. It was he who had sought me out a few weeks after my first visit here.

He appeared unannounced one day at my office, a nicer office than my very junior position warranted, a small space, true, but which yet possessed a sizable blackboard and a window from which I could look out and look down at all the daunting architecture from the vantage point of the seventh floor, where the brightest luminaries of our department were gathered, two laureates and those who were still in waiting, Dietrich Spencer the first in line, for his work on background radiation.

Spencer's finger-snapping had been of no personal significance, for he had quite clearly taken a shine to me and had seen that I'd gotten an office near to his.

Samuel Mallach did not have an office on the starry seventh.

I was very much surprised to see the apparition at my door, who entered with an apology on his lips for interrupting me, while I stood confounded, to find that the author of that astonishing paper had sought me out, his manner to me incongruously respectful, as if he did not know who I was, that I was the most junior member of the department with which he had been associated for longer than I'd been alive.

His manner to me was thus very puzzling, as I respectfully waited for him to speak, and there followed nothing but a long, dismaying silence, finally broken by his faltering voice.

— *You're interested in an objective model for quantum mechanics.*

— *I'm interested in your model.*

Another silence, not quite so long as the first, until he spoke again.

— *There is no collapse in a closed system. No collapse occurs, unless a system interacts with another.*

I assumed he spoke, of course, of the subatomic situation. It was a more than natural assumption, under the circumstances, both his and mine.

— *An interaction between two systems: such as a measurement, you mean.*

At my words, he stood up and excused himself for having disturbed me, shaking my hand and then leaving as abruptly as he had appeared.

A week or so later, he came again, this time staying longer. He stood at my office blackboard and worked out, for my bemused benefit, some not terribly difficult equations. When he was gone I stared a long while at the pale trails of chalk dust he had left behind, then slowly went over to erase some misplaced symbols, correcting the error that he had made.

The next time he came he seemed less tentative and vague, and as he was leaving he turned back to me, as if as an afterthought, and invited me to his home for dinner.

— *It's only my daughter and I. She's probably about your own age. I have a daughter named Dana, you know.*

I knew.

— *Who are you?*

— *Dana Mallach.*

— *His daughter, then.*

— *Yes, his daughter, yes.*

She sat and hardly spoke throughout the dinner, while some quiet woman put down plates of food and later took them away again, disappearing through a soundless swinging door that led to the kitchen. His daughter hardly spoke a word, but she listened raptly, a rapture of attention I could not fathom in the least. I was perplexed that she should turn a face so suffused with unidentifiable emotion onto the cold hard topics on which we spoke, a girl whose light was of some different world, striking imbalance and wild awe wherever it fell. It hardly seemed conceivable, nor, even less so, desirable, that such a girl, who looked to dwell in regions even more remote than a pharaoh's daughter, could take so fervent an interest in the subjects on which her father and I discoursed, for we talked on and on into the small hours of the day.

He did more speaking than I that night, transforming himself, in the process, into a model of inspired lucidity. There was nothing vague and halting about Mallach that night. His very voice was altered, less stiff and more informal, as it traced the hidden life of the electron, and unpacked the meaning of the wave function and the meaning of its collapse.

She did not utter a word of her own, but even so I noticed that her father looked as much at her as he did at me, as if he were concerned that she should understand him, too. I did not guess at all how much she really understood, and thought he looked at her only from fatherly habit, or because it was hard for any human eyes not to seek out the vision of her that night. She was ravishing to the sight.

Her eyes were filled with strange lights, as she rested them on her father and on me, but mostly on him. A girl of furious light beyond the dullish silver of the candleglow, for there had been candles as well as flowers set out, a grand occasion made of it, with goblets that sparkled as if there were diamond dust mixed in the glass. Dana was wearing a dress of wine-colored velvet with a thin velvet ribbon tied around her long white neck, and the gleams and shadows played over the velumen softness as she moved. She carried up green bottles from the cellar, blowing dust and laughing as she decanted the good old wines, euphoric before she had tasted a drop, her eyes dwelling on her father as he descanted on the properties of light.

I could not guess at all at how much she understood of what we spoke, and could not guess that she had tried to do what it was that I had done, to turn his thoughts back again to his physics, as I had done, intent as I was to get the glorious physics out from him. For it was, in the end, only Justin Childs, and I am Justin Childs, who had reminded Mallach of what it was he had lost and what he might regain.

He spoke and spoke that night, all languor and faltering gone, the voice that had drifted like lost gray smoke now vibrating with bright tints and hard intensities, as, tirelessly, he rhapsodized on the search after truth as we physicists know it.

— *The world as it really is, after all, the world as it really is.*

That is how he put it.

— *To turn away from the shadows on the back cave wall, to step out from inside the cave and see the world as it really is, after all.*

He gestured with his hands in motions that were fluid and somehow beautiful. The movements of youth and beauty were preserved in his flowing hands.

— *And we who do it must subdue our subjectivity.*

Her face was caught in some mystery of ardor above the play of candlelight.

— *Subdue ego and error and irrelevance of every kind. It isn't easy, it's a hard day's work, a hard life's. And then the bastards make it even harder.*

His speech abruptly lurched, turning sharply away from rhapsodizing his love to denouncing those he hated, for Mallach's hatred was as intense as anything else he had ever thought or felt. He hated those who had frozen him out, who had closed ranks around their chosen dogmas and frozen him and his hidden variables out.

— *Professor Childs, I'll tell you something very funny. This will make you laugh.*

He turned full face to me, and a darker, more lugubrious cast I could not have imagined.

— *You know, when I first did it, when I first worked out my objective model for q.m., I couldn't believe that I would be the one to see it, that it was me, Samuel Mallach, who was destined to change how everyone thought about the elementary particles of matter. I knew that I was a cracked vessel to hold the truth, but there it was. I had it. I knew there would be controversy. Controversy and fisticuffs is what I expected. After all, Bohr and his pack had gone way out on a limb with their complementarity dogma and what all. They had gone way, way out. But the last thing in the world I ever expected was to be ignored. That wasn't even represented in my calculus of possible outcomes. I thought that it was only the objective merits of the work itself that mattered, especially in science. If not in science, then where else? I thought that everyone would just evaluate what a man had done on the basis of how good it was, how closely it approximated to the truth. I didn't know how things really work in this world, how it gets decided what should be paid attention to, that it's all rigged, the whole system rigged. The big shots decide and the little shots just march lock-stepped into line. It's the machers who have the last word. That was what my father used to say, whether he was talking about the politics in the little synagogue in downtown Scranton, or about Stalin and Roosevelt. "The machers are no mallachs," they're no angels. It was one of his jokes. You see, in Hebrew "mallach" means angel.*

— *And machers?*

— *The makers. The big shots. How would you translate it, Dana?*

— *The machers? Mmm, they're the movers and the shakers, Daddy.*

— *That's right, the movers, the shakers, the loud noisemakers. And they're no mallachs. My father was right. When I was growing up I never paid any attention to what he said. I figured he didn't know anything at all since he didn't understand the first thing about science. But it was me who was the ignoramus. I was completely ignorant in the ways of the world. The machers are no mallachs. If they had attacked me I could have responded to them, I could have answered each one of their objections. I was ready for them. The whole time I was waiting for my paper to come out I was getting ready for the big fights. But they were too smart for that. Why should they have to go through all the hard work of trying to disprove me when they could just as effectively finish me off by ignoring me? Far more effectively finish me off. Here's something else you might find funny, Professor Childs.*

That I very much doubted. I already had reason to suspect his forecasts as to my amusement.

— *Do you know that I seem sometimes to have only one strong emotion left, only one true passion, and that's hatred? Hatred for the forces that have destroyed so many lives, including mine.*

— *Daddy, you're not destroyed, don't say that you're destroyed.*

— *I am, Dana. I am destroyed. Relative to what I could have been, I am destroyed.*

When he spoke like this, of his hatred and his despair, then the bliss fled from her face, all the warm colors bled from her

face, and her eyes went pleadingly in search of mine, in wordless language, imploring that I must help him, stop up the
embittered contents of his soul.

It was as if I heard her speaking directly into my innermost
mind, and in answer to her silent appeal I broached the formidable problem. He, of course, immediately understood the
problem I was indicating: the necessity of relativizing his
model for q.m., of showing it to be Lorentz-invariant and
thereby reconciling relativity theory with quantum mechanics, the fundamental nub being this:

Relativity and quantum mechanics, each of which pre-
cipitated a major conceptual revolution, cognitively clash
with each other. Both can beautifully cover the phenomena
that come directly under them: in the case of quantum mechanics, the elementary particles of matter; in the case of
relativity, the four-dimensional manifold of space-time. But
when they are brought together, as they must eventually be
brought — matter being situated, after all, in the domain of
space-time — the covering fabric is rent unintelligible, and
hideous absurdities invade.

Mallachian mechanics seems, at first blush, more irreconcilable with relativity theory than other formulations of
quantum mechanics, as the very few physicists who had
bothered to take notice of his work had emphasized. But this
is only because it brings out into the light what the other formulations obscure, which is the utterly startling, but nonetheless utterly undeniable fact that nature is, in the word
of the physicist, "nonlocal": events can have instantaneous
influences on other, far-distant events. A crude way of seeing that nonlocality — and therefore quantum mechanics —
is at odds with Einstein's relativity theory is to remember
that it is fundamental to relativity that nothing can travel
faster than light, whereas these instantaneous propagations

of influence seem to indicate superluminal, in fact infinite, velocities. The cognitive dissonance can be expressed in far more subtle and technical terms, involving the relativistic condition of Lorentz invariance, which, when conjoined with quantum nonlocality, allows for such unacceptable anomalies as "backwards causation," which would be the future's affecting the past.

Einstein pursued, through all his last sad years, his elusive dream of a "unified field theory" that would comfortably embrace both q.m. and relativity, and it was in something like the spirit of Einstein's last dream that I broached with Mallach our possibly embarking on the search for the final reckoning.

He understood, of course, that the dissolution of the difficulty of reconciling the two monumental theories of twentieth-century physics required nothing less than the solution of the problem of time, the final explanation of how a correlate of illusive nonrelativistic time appears to be caught up in the quantum situation known as entanglement: systems becoming so enmeshed with one another that the question of their distinct wave functions can no longer be meaningfully raised; only the wave function of their union can be defined. He understood precisely what was entailed in my posing the possibility that he and I, complementarily joined, might together approach the formidable problem, leaping like Empedocles to emerge, both of us, divine.

— *The solution would have to be very deep, and I know it would be very beautiful. I can't see the form it will take yet, but I know it would be very beautiful.*

At these last words of mine, he pushed himself back from the table, his one thin leg crossed over the other, his right elbow poised on his knee and his chin resting in the open palm. He did not speak for five minutes or more, as Dana watched him and I watched them both.

— *Well.*

That was all he said, and he drew it out like an endless sigh.

— *Well.*

As one might sigh above a grave.

Then for several moments more we all three sat, each stupefied on thoughts, until he looked over the brilliance of crystal and candles at his own vision of a girl and smiled sadly at her. His smile was one of his saddest expressions, and there passed the slightest nod across the table from him to her and back from her to him, some transmission of information moving between them faster than the speed of light, like tachyons streaking across the dining room table, and I watched.

Only then did he seem to remember me again, and he smiled at me, not quite so sadly as at her.

— *I will think about what you have said, Professor Childs. You will think and I will think. Perhaps the work you have in mind for us is possible. Perhaps it is even still possible for me. Though I am old with wandering.*

There issued a short sound, something like a laugh, vanishing before I could quite ascertain if a laugh was what it had been.

— *Do you know the poem? The poem by Yeats?*

I shook my head.

— *You must read Yeats. You must read Blake, Justin Childs. Tell him, Dana.*

She laughed, the full range of her rapture all at once now rekindled, and repeated the words of her father obediently.

— *You must read Yeats, you must read Blake, Justin Childs.*

It was the first time she had pronounced my name. I could never have known what it would be like to hear my own name coming out from between her parting lips, *Justin Childs*, when I am Justin Childs.

— *No, no, the poem. Recite the poem for him.*

She looked at me, turning her strange rapt attention full on me, and she shrugged her velveted shoulders and colored in self-consciousness. I had thought myself gone as far as I could go, but at the sight of the wine flush spreading down over the skin that the velvet of her dress had left bare, I went still further.

Softly and solemnly, like a good schoolgirl, she began to recite, because he had requested it of her, the words of the poem:

> *Though I am old with wandering*
> *Through hollow lands and hilly lands,*
> *I will find out where she has gone,*
> *And kiss her lips and take her hands;*
> *And walk among long dappled grass,*
> *And pluck till time and times are done*
> *The silver apples of the moon,*
> *The golden apples of the sun.*

He said nothing more after that, and did not sigh his grave-side sigh, but pushed himself from the table, this time unfolding his long and wasted body and slowly rising. Without a word he kissed her good night on her forehead, and then held her at arm's length for several moments more, staring at the spot he had just kissed. He kissed her again on each of her eyes, and turned to me, offering a limp and silent handshake, his hands now gone old. I thanked him for the night, he smiled, shook my hand again, just as limply, and left the room.

She told me to wait, she would be back in several minutes, and she followed him out. I heard them climbing the long swirling stairway together, their quiet voices covered at last in the measured heavy silence.

I was in a problematic state, a state of body as well as of mind, a steady pounding in the blood and subtle body.

These are sensations I cannot recall with perfect clarity and calm, and, with just so little clarity and calm, I sat and waited for the reappearance of the girl.

She came to the door and motioned silently for me to follow her.

I could not bear to end the night, though I had no thought that I might prolong it through any effort of my own. I was just as passive as I was pounding, and I dreaded, in my problematic state, to leave the house on Bagatelle Road, just as I dreaded to stay, for I knew to stay would be terrible, but not so terrible as to leave. The world outside her sphere was suddenly given to me in all its drabness and all its coldness, the world as it really is, after all, the world as it really is, so that I wondered how I would from now on bear it, live and yet not feel it, and wondered how it was that I had lived until now, what had I thought of and what had I felt?

She did not lead me to the door, but past the door and up the swirling stairs.

I followed mutely after, as I'd followed her father that first autumn afternoon, and I followed her down the haunted corridor that led us to this room, it is Dana's room, where we sat facing each other on this bed, it is Dana's bed.

She took off her shoes and they dropped soundlessly onto the thick white carpet, and I told her, so unlike me but for the pounding motions in my blood, of the fingers of my light, how they had pierced my telescope's clear lens to probe the dim, dark bodies splayed gently onto the night.

She listened with a look half-serious and not, sitting back on her feet so that she was kneeling, her knees just barely touching mine, and she reached out both hands and took my glasses off, placing them carefully on this little table. I did not gasp aloud, I do not think, not quite aloud, but I kissed her lips, and took her hands and kissed them, too, and tried to kiss her lips again, but she turned them away, and I was mortally afraid, for a split second of eternity, that I had done something wrong to turn her from me.

She had a look both serious and not, I could not quite get hold of it, as she took hold of the fingers of my hand, and she traced them with her own long index finger, the up and the down of the wavelets of my hand, so that it was the fingers of my hand that went to fire, and she took them in her mouth, one after the other, between those softly parting lips, *mmm*, she whispered, her mouth against my ear, *fingers of light*, with a look both serious and not, my fingers reaching for the knowledge of her, moving over her cheeks, her neck, her mouth, and she pretended that they burned her tongue, taking them into her softly opening mouth, *fingers of light*, her words against my ear, and with the fingers of my hand she led me to the otherness of her, it was a different Dana, to see such a Dana emerging from behind the other, to see the thing her body really was, how unafraid she was, stepping into the fire to emerge divine, Dana divine and taking me in, her body arched upward like a flame above my own, fierce at one moment, tender at the next, her tenderness was the most terrible aspect of it all, I did not know if I would emerge from it at all.

— *Close your eyes Dana for pity's sake close your eyes for pity's sake I am dying against the glass beating helpless on the glass while you stare at me unmoved.*

Gazing at me from out of the ice blue stillness of her unforgiving eyes, not a motion of pity to disturb the hard, smooth surface of her stare, a different Dana, a frightening unknown.

— For pity's sake Dana pity me please pity me.

My two fists blackening while they beat against the glass and the icy flames roared up and through me, paradox abounding, even in death, for I was turning to ice through the agency of fire, caught fast inside the flaming car, which she had driven and she had crashed, her cold voice relentlessly cataloguing the reasons for her hatred.

— It was you who destroyed him. Not my mother. Not me. Only you, Justin Childs.

And I am Justin Childs, crushed and caught in metal, beating blackened against the glass, while on the other side stands my Dana, perfectly still and staring, hesitating the long fiery seconds that would have saved me.

— For pity's sake for pity's sake why can't you pity me as I'd pity you?

The knowledge come at last, the answer written plainly in her terrible eyes.

Through hollow lands and hilly lands.

I will find out where she has gone.

VI

The universe might ultimately be — there is some evidence — coherent.

But it is also, and just as rigorously, cold. There are equations at the heart of it, but they are written out in a frozen · fire, and the heart at the heart of the heart includes no sense at all of anything remotely resembling pity.

Such was the world according to Dana Mallach, who held that reality was both deeply rational and just as deeply unmoved, and she claimed to have had the gist of this truth from as far back as she could remember.

"Even when I was the smallest child, Justin. Of course I hadn't possessed the language for expressing what it was I so absolutely knew. Instead I had all those sleep problems."

Every night, she had wandered the house, arising two or three times before dawn to leave the frilly white bedroom at the end of the long black corridor, her dilated pupils frantically sifting the dark for intruders, flesh or phantom. She would pad softly on her bare feet the long way to her parents' bedroom, never awakening them, at least never intentionally. She would open the door, inch by inch so that it would not creak, wanting only to see that they were there, that they were safe, that they had not fallen victim to the hideous possibilities that ought not, for pity's sake, to have been possible at all, though she knew that they were, it was the gist of the truth. She wanted only to observe without disturbing, validating that they were untouched, for the time being unharmed.

Dana still described her childhood terrors to Justin with palpable anguish, and he would listen with both tenderness and respect, for Justin had never experienced anything like these early vastations. The world, to the child of him that he had been, had seemed as straightforwardly self-evident as his meticulously constructed truth tables for first-order logic. *Every proposition is either true or false, and no proposition is both!* It had never occurred to him, as a boy, to imagine the worst.

"That just proves I was a much more imaginative child than you were, my poor Justin."

She smiled up at him, so seraphically that he knew for certain she meant him a slight.

"I was plenty imaginative as a kid," he answered her, while seizing a fistful of her light-spun hair and holding it hard away from her face. He could see the skin being pulled up near her temples. She did not flinch, though her eyes shone too bright, and he let the fistful drop.

"Mmm, of course you were. We were both amazing children, there's no question. Only your brilliance expressed itself in fabulously untrue theories and mine took the form of sleep problems. You were brilliantly in error and I was brilliantly insomniac."

It was Justin now who barely slept, while Dana slept lightly beside him. Justin had learned how to still himself relentlessly, so that even in his sleep he never stirred even the most minor of muscles beside her. He often stayed up half the night watching her closed eyes, watching as they shivered over dreams.

— *Do you dream of me, Dana?*

And if she said *yes*, could he then have been happy? Could she be believed? She had an inner life, that was the sorry truth. She had a mind, and it was the source of his absolute uncertainty. It was a torment to need so desperately to know the contents of her mind, the hidden variables behind her words and silences and laughter, the varieties of intent behind her murmured mmm's.

Justin had never known anyone as mind-proud as Dana. Mind-proud as other women are house- or husband-proud. It was just like her to dress up even her early-childhood phobias so that they took on the brilliance of infant metaphysics, to drape elaborate ratiocinations over her spooks. It was so very like Dana to deform her early neurosis into puerile prescience that sometimes Justin found himself, in the very act of disbelieving Dana's version of herself, loving her all the better for her fabulations, for her need for these, childlike and vain.

But there were other times when he became impatient with the hidden strain of irrationality that ran through her thoughts like a poison through her system, the soured metaphysics she had imbibed from her earliest hours, from her mother, who had been a drunk. It was when her vagaries seemed to bear the taint of Dotty that Justin couldn't abide them. Everything that he had managed to learn about her dead and much-loved mother offended him, the sort of woman, silly-drunk on vanity, who drew the bitter ire from the sweetness of his mother. His mother had wasted no pity on women like Dotty.

Dotty had carried her drunken death within her like a softening fruit, even though she'd been no simple drunk, possessing spiritual leanings that had set the light craft of her mind to list. Would they had gone down with her, those obscure longings for the light, would they had died a full and fitful death in Dotty.

The faculty of disbelief in Dotty had gotten jammed, and everything was getting through. She had been an epistemological calamity. The distinction between truth and falsity had been misplaced, she had forgotten the difference altogether, until death itself made the indifference complete.

A portrait of the mother manqué and her very young daughter, done in oils, reigned above the mantel of the library fireplace, Dotty staring off into a distant place from where she might have imagined her slanted illumination to derive. His own mother would have stared at him and not at the mystic faraway.

He could not but know what a mother is meant to be. Bent at an awkward angle over the red Formica of the kitchen counter in the early evening shadowing of winter, spreading the Fluff and peanut butter onto spongy bread, the worn leather of the French volume at her pudgy elbow, her eyes lustering at each protracted tremor in the echoing chambers of Marcel's lacerated, overworked heart.

Dotty was made to be mocked. He wished for Dana to mock at her in unison with him. Their voices joined in sweetest mockery would have made a music he might love. Husband and daughter, in their bereavement (groundless), made the woman over into a false guise. Mallach was grotesquely mawkish on the subject of his dead wife.

"My wife was a most extraordinary manner of woman," he had told Justin the day that he had danced out the motions of light for him. They had walked through a frozen field, circling round and round a famous pond, its surface going from silver to lead to iodine as the winter's early dusk drew in.

It was only Justin and Mallach, Dana having stayed at home, and there was an Olympian loftiness to their stride that day, a day of glorious physics.

They had caught a glimpse of the form of forms, and the subsiding bliss left Mallach in an exalted mood of revelation, so that he had spoken to Justin of her, of his dead wife.

"She made me suffer horribly, you know. She drove me to the brink and even over, and I was grateful to her for it. I owe my best ideas in science to my life with Carlotta."

Justin had stared at Mallach, groping for words through his sense of uneasy disbelief.

"You owe your scientific ideas to her? But she wasn't a physicist. She didn't know any science."

"No, Justin, you misunderstand. It was in my life with her, in its intensity. That was what made it possible for me to think as I did in those days. I'll never be able to think with the same intensity again."

Mallach saw the woman as a seeker of their sort, when she was not. He could not see her as clearly as Justin saw. How did Justin know they falsified their Dotty if he had never met her living? How could he be so certain? He was. Insubstantial as she was, she still left marks behind that Justin, at least, could read.

He had no doubt. Her books alone revealed the fool she'd been, the drunken, soft-brained fool. *The Tibetan Book of the Dead, Tantra and the Sacred Fire, Madame Blavatsky Still Speaks, Meditation for the Muddled Masses, for the Huddled That Have Gone to Muddled Masses.*

Meditation, requiring as it does a process of sustained concentration, he imagined would have been infinitely beyond her, though he gathered that she had mastered so well the Zen art of emptying her mind that it became for her a state constant and involuntary.

She was a drunk. She died a drunk. She drove her car into a township tree, and left her daughter motherless at nine.

"My mother died too, you know."

She said this once, quite coldly. It was only once out of all the many times that he had spoken to her of Schubert's *Unfinished* and the drunk who had come hurtling out of the configuration space of possibilities to dislodge his parents from his world.

He had dreamed night and day that a fairy girl would turn to him and speak, in the language of pity and with the voice of an answering angel, and he would tell her and she would know.

"My mother died too, you know. I realize it was both your parents, which is unspeakably tragic, but still, I was very young, far younger than you."

"Are we comparing tragedies now? Are we going to compete here, too?"

"It's not a matter of competing, Justin. My God, how odd that you'd even think it was. It's just that there's something in your way of speaking of it to me that seems oblivious to the fact that I lost my mother, too."

"No, Dana. No. It's not the same. My mother was killed by a drunk. Your mother was the drunk. She might have killed someone else. Have you ever thought of that? She might have killed someone else that night."

"But she didn't. No one died that night but she."

"But someone else could have. That's not irrelevant. You seem to think it's irrelevant, Dana. Admit to me that it's not."

Dana looked away, her blaze extinguished, though she had been so fierce the moment before, a girl of furious light, she said nothing more now, so that he knew that there was more.

"What is it? What did she do?"

Dana would not look at him. He could not bend that ray to meet his own.

"Don't try to hide it from me, Dana. You know that you can't do it."

"There was someone else with her in the car."

She spoke very quietly, still looking away. He could not bend her.

"Who? Was it you?"

"No, not me, and not my father. Someone else. I don't know who. A man."

"Was he killed?"

"No." It was impossible to read the expression off her face at the angle at which she held it away from him. Her voice, too, low and affectless, yielded as little as possible.

"Does your father know who it was?"

"Of course. Of course he knows."

"But he wouldn't tell you?"

She finally looked at Justin, with icy fury, as if she held an accusation out, and her voice came out as an undisguised hiss.

"No, Justin. I would never ask."

Those two were preposterous in grieving her. Foolishness was not disfiguring in Dana, but in Samuel Mallach it was grotesque. He was a quantum genius. He was a consummate fool.

"My wife was a most extraordinary manner of woman."

No, she had been nothing of the kind, you poor deluded cuckold. That was what Justin would have loved to declare, in that darkening field, with a Mallach gone blasphemously silly. There is nothing extraordinary in the least in a vain and dimwitted woman making far too much of herself and inducing others to do the same.

Justin knew about these things from Proust. He knew about the sufferings that the worthless Odette, whom his mother had despised, had inflicted on the connoisseur of beauty, M. Swann. Swann had overlaid the shallowness of Odette with qualities that were entirely of his own making. Justin knew all about Carlotta Mallach from Odette de Crécy, the vilest creature, his mother had told him, in the entire seven volumes of À la recherche du temps perdu. Cynthia Childs had hurled harsh epithets at Odette in her girlishly sweet voice. She had called her a man-eater. She had called her a slut.

It angered Justin that both Mallach and his daughter got that dotty woman so consistently wrong. (He called her Dotty to himself, a Childsish joke, he called it that, too.)

"I owe my best ideas in science to my life with Carlotta," Mallach had declared, and Justin had not known whether to laugh or cry at the extravagant pathos of his tone.

Dotty's books were sacred relics in this house. In the library, there is still a shelf reserved for Dotty's tomes.

Dana had stood across the room from him, beside this window. It was winter. There was a noisy fire going, its crepitation syllabizing the angry silence.

They were vexed with each other, they had argued. They were both in a mood to be cruel. Justin saw the set of her mouth and read the coldness gathered in her eyes, and he wanted to strike the certainty out from her. He could feel the desire glowing at the ends of his hands. She seemed grotesquely her mother's daughter, garishly fatuous, an unforgivable distraction from their work. He told her this, precisely, and saw her stare back, stricken.

"Your mother had her try at destroying your father, she gave it her best, and now it's your turn."

All semblance of certainty vanished, she stared back, ravished, his beautiful girl again. But he still was not appeased, somehow there was a lag in his appeasement.

He seized a random volume from the Dotty shelf, releasing a soft dense flurry of tiny white slips, wingless birds in flight, spiraling downward from between the vapid lines. Dana let out a strangled cry, so unlike her it was chilling and nearly tragic. He was appeased, though it was too late, for she was already sinking onto her knees in a heart-rending motion, so that he was more than appeased, he wished for it to stop, which it did not, and in the midst there of Dotty's tumbling topics, she cried out aloud:

"No!"

Stooped down to gather them up, illegible as they were,

cupping them in her chaliced palms, she was inconsolable at the disarrangement of deranged jottings.

Still, he could not forgive the husband and daughter their grieving. They made Dotty out to be a largeness largely unknown, but what they took for the murkiness of depths was only a drunkenness of the soul. Zen and theosophy; astrology and numerology; tarot cards and Madame Blavatsky; electromagnetic diets and communications with the dead. It was all a form of drunkenness in her. Dana's mother had taken her eight-year-old daughter to a séance and scared the child almost as witless as she. Dana mentioned it to him once, though soon regretted it. He tried to dig the details out from her, and she grew sullen.

"You're saying that she took you with her to those ridiculous hoaxes? A child who could never sleep through a night? Or did your sleep problems only start after being dragged by your mother to these entertainments?"

"I've always had problems sleeping."

"But not anymore."

She was angry and wouldn't answer, but still it was true. With Justin beside her, Dana Mallach could at last submit to sleep and he would lie beside her and watch her dream.

Do you dream of me, Dana?

VII

He woke up to astonishment.

Dana was shaking him, her hand at his bare shoulder and ungentle. He had been vividly dreaming of her only the moment before. His astonishment was such now that he barely knew whether he dreamed or not.

He half sat up, supporting himself on his elbows, and gazed up stupidly at her. She was already dressed, wearing gray wool trousers and two soft blue sweaters, one with buttons over one without, a matching set.

Her hair was still damp from her shower, and he could smell her shampoo. The smell of it was so mysterious and of her that it pierced him through and through. The color of her sweaters corresponded to the color of her eyes with a precision that also affected him too deeply.

He would have liked it if she had smiled at him in the morning light. He wasn't certain if they were friends, if they had become friends at all in the course of the night.

"You'll have to hurry, Justin. I have breakfast with my father every morning. He's downstairs waiting, so please hurry and I'll wait for you."

These were the first words she spoke to him after the transfigurations of the night before, and he found them disturbing, unworthy, wrong.

"Can't I shower?"

His own first words to her sounded wrong, too — like a clumsy translation of what he had meant to say.

She glanced at the clock on her white night table.

"If you take no more than ten minutes altogether to get ready."

Her tone was sharp and cold, and it struck him as awful. She seemed an arbitrary manner of person to him then. He disliked people who insisted without cause, people who pushed forward their chosen trivialities as if they were laws of nature.

But then perhaps she was rather an arbitrary manner of person. Perhaps she was even awful. She was a pharaoh's daughter and might very well be quite awful. He didn't really know. He didn't know her at all. He had come the night before to speak of physics with her father, and she had listened with a strange rapture of attention, and she had taken him upstairs and to her bed and now here he was.

Had he only dreamed the transformations of last night, then? Had he only dreamed the tenderness of Samuel Mallach's daughter?

The words she had whispered with her mouth against his ear, the soft breaths and sighs and secrets she had told him in the movements that were love: dreams?

He knew that he had dreamed, that just before he had been shaken awake by her ungentle hand he had been lost in a swirling rivulet of dreams.

"I'll wait for you on the landing," she said, and this he accepted in gratitude as an act of kindness. He would never have been able to bring himself to climb out, in front of this Dana, a different Dana from the night before, from beneath the bedcovers, where he lay naked. She traversed thought processes that did not correspond in any way to his own and he did not know her in the least.

In the shower, he found himself thinking of his mother. Beneath the tapestry of nighttime sky she had told him stories to go with the stars, and many of them had been of lovers.

On those nights when it was just the two of them, his mother and he had indulged themselves in seeing constellations of their own choosing. In eight stars that appeared in the northern quadrant of the winter skies of Olympia, they had seen the enchanted ladder of the fairy girl's hair. In four dim stars they had found the prince who had scrambled up the ladder to find his pleasure. His love had deceived him and he had fallen down and been blinded by two thorns.

They picked out the stars that were the thorns in his eyes. They picked out the face hid amid a crowd of stars.

He lost track of the time, and then he had to dress in a hurry, putting on the clothes he had worn to dinner the night before, anxious that Dana might no longer be waiting for him, even though she had promised.

He found her standing with her back toward the mirror on the stairwell landing, where he had seen her face the first time in reflection. Wordlessly, they went together to join her father.

Samuel Mallach sat at the unclothed table, wide bands of brilliant sunshine falling in from the two windows behind him, catching the grain of the dark shining wood, strands of his limp gray hair lit to silver. He was frowning, intently putting marmalade on toast. He registered no surprise at all to see their dinner guest from the night before still with them, entering the dining room in the same suit and shirt and tie as he'd worn the evening before.

The door from the kitchen opened, and the silent woman who had brought them their food the night before now carried out a plate of toast, nodding wordlessly at Dana, her eyes darting to Justin and then away.

Samuel Mallach continued to spread his toast, very precisely and evenly, an activity that lasted in silence for several minutes. Finally, the task of toast completed, he turned to look at them both, studying first his daughter and then their visitor.

"I've been thinking about quantum nonlocality since last night," he finally announced.

Justin, who had never before awakened in a girl's home and

in her bed, much less been forced to go down in the morning and take breakfast with her father, who was the physicist he admired the most in all the world, could not have been better pleased with this salutation, with its promise that Mallach and he would take up their discussion of the night before.

"Mmm, so have I," Dana answered her father. She had been served eggs by the silent woman. "What about you, Justin? Have you been thinking about nonlocality as well?"

Justin looked up from the plate of scrambled eggs that had been put at his own place. Samuel Mallach alone had been served no eggs. Dana was looking at him as she waited for him to answer. Although she was not unambiguously smiling, there was a slant to her mouth that looked possibly like hidden laughter. Justin was not confident, but it might be laughter.

"A little," he said in a noncommittal tone. "Yes, maybe a little."

"So you see we've all been thinking about nonlocality, which is something like nonlocality itself. Nonlocality of mind."

It was Dana who said this, and a fork skewering some egg stopped right before Justin's mouth. Dana's words were so extravagantly unexpected that he wondered if he had heard them quite as she had meant them. Before he could pursue the question in his own mind, her father spoke again.

"And, you, Professor Childs, do you believe that nature is nonlocal?"

Justin turned to stare at Mallach. Quantum nonlocality is the feature whereby particles, having once been subjected to quantum entanglement, will forever after continue to assert, even when widely separated, instantaneous influences over one another. It is a feature that, however counterintuitive and mysterious — not to speak of incompatible with relativity theory — it might appear to be, is a consequence of realistically interpreting the theory.

Justin cleared his throat, pondering the motivation behind Mallach's question, a confoundedly naïve-seeming query to be issuing from the man who last night had drawn forth the intimate secrets of particles and light, and had appeared to presume a certain level of understanding on the part of his invited guest.

"Yes, of course I think nature is nonlocal. How could I think otherwise, in light of your own objective formulation? The only alternative is the radical nonsense of the subjectivists."

"Do you think so? Dana thinks something very similar."

Justin was distracted by some movement to his right. A cup was filling up with steaming dark liquid. Coffee. He looked up and saw the silent woman — her name was Dora, Dana and her father always said it, *Thank you, Dora* — standing to his right, holding a silver urn from which she was pouring coffee into his cup.

"Not something very similar," Dana was saying to her father as Justin watched the coffee streaming from on high into his cup. Wasn't the woman afraid that it might splatter him? He glanced up at her and saw that her face was disagreeably set. She looked like she might well be intending to scald him. Or perhaps it just seemed so from the angle of his perception. "Identical."

Justin turned to Dana, whose words shocked him to the core. He had never considered the possibility that this pharaoh's girl might speak the language of the pharaoh; that her thought processes might correspond so closely to his own.

He had not known in his life a single girl who knew anything of significance in science. The tanned young beauties who had pedaled slowly past him on their bikes in Paradise,

California, had never brought their slanting rays of light with them into the rooms where he had studied the laws of matter in motion, where he had studied the four-dimensional manifold of relativistic space-time.

Still, there were grounds yet remaining to doubt that Dana truly knew anything of physics, that she grasped the real nature and intent of the words she threw off so lightly while reconfiguring the scrambled eggs laid out on her plate.

"Nonlocality is merely the expression of quantum entanglement," she said, further eroding the grounds for doubt. Had she any more idea of what "entanglement" meant than she had of "nonlocality"? Her statement enclosed a gloriously sweeping insight, the scope of it nearly taking Justin's breath away, but was it, in any way, hers? Was she claiming it for her own? She might be repeating words she had heard, as a child does, producing the bizarre effect of infant brilliance.

"That's rather beautifully put, Dana," her father said. "That's very fine poetry. It's finely put, but is it true?"

Justin turned from the daughter to the father and then back again to her. But she did not return his gaze, though he focused all his thought on seeing through to her true nature. She appeared indifferent to his stare, her face in profile to him, her hair still slightly damp and darkened. She was gazing steadfastly at her father, the wide bands of sharp light turning the air around him into a glowy haze, the dust particles alit and dancing out their frenzied motions, the explanation of which had eventually won Einstein his highest prize. The Swedes had played it safe, granting him their recognition for the light he had shed on the dance of dust, rather than for his laying bare the structure of four-dimensional space-time.

"What is that poem I'm thinking of, Dana? You know the one I mean. How did that other poet put it?"

"All things linked are. Thou canst not stir a flower, without troubling of a star."

In the morning light, she quoted the poetry he demanded from her without blushing to the color of wine. She spoke it as if to get it out of the way.

"What do you think of that, Justin? It's also finely put, but is it true? Is it a consequence of our quantum reality?"

Justin looked from the father to the daughter and then back again to him.

"Don't you like eggs?"

He was surprised himself to hear the question he asked.

"My heart is bad," Mallach answered.

VIII

— *I've been thinking.*

I despaired in general when she spoke those words.

— *The wave function* —

— *Yes!*

Her father's attention instantaneously fled from the difficult question before us, bolting like a wild animal that had been held against its will.

I had been demonstrating for them some lovely math, and remonstrating, too. It baffled me how people could resist math's gorgeousness, but people did, and people do. The fire of its purity drives them away, the purity of the fire, unmixed with the heaviness of unnecessitated being. Dana would flutter her hands and look elsewhere, and even Mallach could become as impatient with the intricacies of signs and abstractions, as obdurately uncomprehending, as one of his own physics-for-poets nonpoets.

She had been chewing distractedly on a pencil for a good half an hour, the unendurably beautiful eyes unfixed on what I had to show. We sat in the room where the late-afternoon light entered through Carlotta's wall of glass. A long triangle of light lay on the small round table where we three sat working, a cup of green tea gone cold near Dana's elbow. It was a warm midsummer's day, and Dana had piled her pale hair onto her head and worn a short dress of sunshine yellow that looked like something a six-year-old might wear to go outside and skip rope down the street. We three had a child's chalkboard set up between us, and Dana had her lined yellow pad balancing on her lap, and around the central truth of Mallachian mechanics, she was triangularly doodling. She doodled often and these were her chosen figures, so that she had cast a net of threaded triangles over her father's guiding equation.

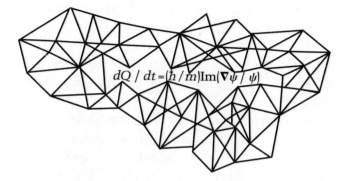

$$dQ / dt = (\hbar / m)\text{Im}(\nabla\psi / \psi)$$

— *I've been thinking* —

— *Yes?*

— *The wave function* —

— *Yes, Dana, what?*

— *Maybe psi is the mathematical expression for mind.*

Eagerness quickened in Mallach's face. A light like lunacy went on in his eyes.

— *Mind in the equations? The psi a symbol for mind? Is that what you mean?*

— *Perhaps, Daddy . . .*

— *Yes?*

— *Perhaps even for the mind of God.*

What was I not up against with those two? He had seemed struck as with a god-sent fire by his daughter's nonsense message. He often was. More struck by her groping vagaries than by my own pyrophoric forms.

No physicist could wield the fire of higher mathematics better than I. The department itself acknowledged this. One or another illustrious physicist would summon me to bring the transformative fire down into a cold and inert physical description.

Mallach's foot often tapped out the rhythm of his impatience as I would try to unwind for him the long looping strands of incandescent math. But at some loopy thought of hers the all of him went rapt, and he slipped over, before one knew it, falling headlong into rapture.

I loved her, yes, but I did not love these . . . events. I did not love Mallach's being struck as if by the gods with her random ravings. They were searching after truth in all the wrong places, and it would be left for me to haul them back . . . to haul *him* back from such misguided deviations.

Perhaps at such times I felt something even approaching the rivalry of a sibling.

That is an insight on my part, not at all of the sort I am given to considering, and I have only just formed it. I must think a bit on this.

I have thought.

He went unnaturally still and stared at her with such a look as angels look, as angels and the mad.

He's mad, I thought, but I'll still get the physics from him. I'll ward off her dotty contributions, her mind-of-God intrusions, and get the physics out from him.

He had some access more immediate than the ways I knew. I would not have imagined, but for those Mallachs, that there could be any knowledge-bearing faculty more powerful than mathematics: the language of the cold angels.

He told me how it was that he felt the science within himself, in the sensations of his own body. He told me how he could feel the hidden motions of matter as displacements in his own muscles.

It was a darkening afternoon on a winter day that had been winter-bright, fantastic light, and we two circled round and round a little pond that was frozen hard and smooth. He had danced out for me the motions of light in the two-slit experiment, his arms held limply over his gangly body as he moved, as if to keep them from getting caught up in his own long legs.

— We'd need a crowd here to do it right. Then we could arrange them in the right interference patterns, over there, near the woods. We could get the whole high-and-mighty physics department out here, dancing around like a pack of demented photons. Now that would be some fun.

We had finished a wonderful day's work. We had lifted a bit of the heavy veil the material world wears across her face, mysterious and beautiful beyond measure, beyond all the crudities of measure, and caught a feature of a feature never quite so glimpsed before. No one who has never done this can possibly imagine the bliss.

We had demonstrated, in the strictest mathematical terms, an essential fact about the state of knowledge itself: how it is that the knower and the known are physically entangled with one another, the wave function of the one superimposed upon the wave function of the other, and how, therefore, knowledge can itself lead to physically dramatic results: knowledge can wreak astonishments.

There is the system to be known, there is the system that comes to know, and these two systems, once entangled, will forever be susceptible to each other's influence. One of us, perhaps it had been Dana, had summed up the startling truth by calling it the bizarre efficacy of knowledge. Yes, it had been Dana.

We had shaken hard the tree of stars, and one had fallen down and shattered open at our feet, and we could only stare, starstruck and momentarily chastened.

They did not back away from the purifying fire of my math, and I did not resist the intuitions that beckoned them on to the gnosis of the psi, for we had shaken loose a star from the tree of stars.

Dana and I were exhausted, Dana especially, but the effects

of that heightened day on Mallach had been altogether different, and I saw him as he must once have been, a young man and in love, clothed in flame, all the morbidity of his sorrow burned away.

— *Come, children, we'll go for a walk. We'll take a quick walk while there's still some light to catch outside.*

It was early dusk, the dead of winter. There were wild colors in the sky, refraction's grand finale.

Dana declined.

— *I want to sleep. I'm suddenly dead tired. Tell Dora I won't be down for dinner. I want to sleep and sleep and sleep.*

Mallach kissed her on her forehead.

— *You've a right to be tired. You've done good work.*

He said it soft with love, so soft. *My children,* he had said, but he loved her better. It was the natural course of things that he should love her, who was of his own blood, better, and nature here held steady.

My children, he had said, but he loved her better.

Mallach and I had gone striding through the embered remnants of the day, covering the snow-packed ground with our Olympian strides, Mallach opening himself to words of a different sort than I had ever heard him speak before.

— *Einstein once told me that he used to feel the physics inside of him, as well. I remember that. I remember everything about that conversation.*

He struck the personal vein in the late afternoon. In the closing blaze of the late afternoon, he went to stark disclosure. This was unusual for Samuel Mallach, though not because he was a selfless man. His very sorrow was a rapture of self-absorption. His love of truth was nothing impersonal, though the question can certainly be posed whether anyone's is. Zeno Wicks told me once that he would far prefer that an important truth not be discovered at all than that someone other than he should discover it, and Zeno was a paradox only in his self-honesty.

In any case, Mallach loved the truth that he had found because it was the truth that *he* had found. He might have seemed to some, as he did to Dana, to possess the self-transcendence of a saint, but it was only because his egotism was too large to be contained in the first person. It spread itself out in waves of universal abstraction. The angels are no different.

— *I remember everything about that conversation with Einstein. He was old, and I was young, probably younger than you are now.*

I doubted that he knew how old I then was, for he had certainly never asked, and I was quite young for my position.

— *He had the air of an immense sorrow, or so it seemed to me. Frustration and isolation closing out the glory days. We didn't speak of physics but of the possibilities for knowing physics. It was of knowledge itself that we spoke. He told me that he also felt the equations inside his muscles, in sensations that lay deeper down than reason.*

I did not place blind faith in Mallach's account of his conversation with Albert Einstein. For one thing, I could attach no sense to *deeper down than reason*. It is the sort of adverbial clumping indulged in by those who simply cannot think, they don't know how. On the other hand, no one could compellingly make the case that Samuel Mallach was unacquainted with the processes of thought, nor, for that matter, dismiss Albert Einstein as a dummkopf.

Still, I didn't overly trust Mallach's recollections of the day. There were always grounds to distrust Mallach's recall of events. He had lost so many memories and then refound them, and who was to say that, in the process of their dislocation, they had not been subjected to radical deformation or worse? His was a degenerative mental disorder, his chronic case of sorrow, slowly softening all the faculties of his mind, undoing memory, reason and will.

Still, it moved me very much to hear him speak like this. It thrilled a filament in me to a fine rich glow, placing my person in the way of the great chain of knowing, from the Almighty through Einstein and Mallach and threading on down through me.

— *He told me I was the only other physicist he knew of who felt the physics in his own body. Not Bohr or Planck or Born, Pauli, Dirac or Heisenberg. Not even Schrödinger. They none of them felt it in just that way. Dana feels it, too, of course. That you know.*

— *Yes.*

— *I remember when I first set her the problem of the precession of the gyroscope. She must have been about fifteen or sixteen. She knew about conservation of momentum, knew all the relevant formulas, but she still kept coming back to me and saying that she couldn't understand how the gyroscope moves. Show me what you have, I said. She showed me, and she had derived the sort of mechanical solution that would have satisfied almost any professional physicist. But still she was dissatisfied, she said she didn't understand the motions at all, until we were walking here one evening and she was able to imagine herself as a gyroscope, she was able to infiltrate its motions. Only then, she told me, did she understand.*

I didn't like to discuss these sorts of matters with him, having no sympathy for the sort of epistemological romanticism that those two went in for, and I didn't really trust his recollections of Albert Einstein in the least.

— It was a tremendous personal tragedy for me when he died, when Einstein died. He had told several people that he thought of me as his rightful successor. Did you know that?

— Yes. Dana told me.

— Did she?

— Yes.

We had made almost another complete revolution around the frozen pond before he spoke once more.

— So Dana told you, then. He said it to several people. I heard it independently from several colleagues. It was before they turned against me. Before I had done anything of any importance to set them dead against me.

The icy snow crunched crystalline beneath us, we were retracing our own footsteps, the early-falling dusk turning the silvery landscape into lead. It was a few days after Christmas, a black and private anniversary of my own. I thought I knew what was coming next, where Mallach was heading in his solipsistic pathway, an inward spiral of darkening diatribe, ending in the anguished reprisal of his betrayal, the litany of the false friends, of Bildad and Zophar and Eliphaz. The Book of Job was Mallach's favorite text of Scripture, the only one from which he nowadays quoted, though there had been a time when he had known them all. He had been raised in the tradition, Dana spoke of it with a touch of tremble, awed that her paternal grandfather had wrapped himself in a fringed prayer shawl and bound his arms with phylacteries, as even her father had done in his youth. It shocked her more than me to think of him that way, to picture him in the trappings of the devout. To me it never seemed so strange in Mallach, who seemed to me a man of spirit, for better or worse: an em-

bittered spiritualist, a category of person not unknown to reconfigure possibilities and arise to wreak astonishments.

— *It was a tragedy that he died before I'd done my work.
Things would have turned out quite differently for me if
he had lived long enough to see my work. He would have
understood.*

— *Is that true? He had no love for nonlocality. He called it
"spooky action at a distance."*

One could never count on Mallach's faculty of recall.
Would I have to review for him once more the fundamentals
of the Einstein-Podolsky-Rosen Paradox, in which Einstein,
affirming the "separation principle," had ruled against the
possibility of a nonlocal influence — of particles, widely separated, instantaneously affecting the behavior of one another?

— *Of course, of course, but I would have been able to con-
vince him. Einstein was a rational man of science. Eminently rational. All the things they say about him, that as an
old man he couldn't accept the revolutions in thought that
weren't of his own doing and that that's why he never accepted the quantum world? That's all wrong. No correspon-
dence to the truth whatsoever. They can't get anything
about the quantum story straight, not even the personalities
involved, especially when it comes to Einstein. What Einstein couldn't accept was the radical incoherence. My model
would have convinced him. Schrödinger, too. He called nonlocality black magic, didn't he?*

— *Magic. "Measurements on separated systems cannot directly influence each other — that would be magic."*

Mallach laughed, a brief and frigid noise. The sky was almost completely darkened over now. The air was cold and
had gone sweet with the smoke ascending from the rows of
attached residences across the frozen lawn and little road. In-

side those homes were gentle Hestias, house- and husband-proud, and the sweet scent of the smoke they made to warm the ones they loved insinuated an aching tenderness into the cold air seeping into me, as I thought how Dana would never think to make me cocoa, crowned with dollops of Marshmallow Fluff. Perhaps if her father's heart had not been bad, precluding the possibilities for cocoa, then there would be crested cups awaiting us at home.

I wanted cocoa. With all my soul's dim stirrings, I desired hot cocoa with Marshmallow Fluff.

— *I would have convinced them both. Einstein and Schrö-dinger were my two scientific parents. I've always thought of them that way.*

It was getting very cold now, the cruel edge revealing itself in the cold, and we were neither of us wearing gloves, our hands plunged into the pockets of our bulky down jackets, mine a souvenir from my days on the links of old Olympia.

— *A scientist has two family trees. There is the biological one, which is often quite painfully irrelevant. Then there is the scientific one.*

I nodded my agreement beside him, though he could not have seen because his eyes were not on me, and I had the vaguest sense I was eavesdropping once again, as I had done before, when he and his daughter had sat over breakfast, their hushed voices maddeningly just beyond my hearing, like two bad children keeping secrets from a third.

— *Their acceptance would have meant more to me than anything else. I would have been able to take all the jeering from on low. I would have just jeered back. But I never got their approval. They both died too soon for me to get it.*

His tone of voice was unmistakably bitter, and I was resigned to my certainty of where his bitterness was taking him, that the vast waves of his critical judgment would in any instant now collapse into a particle localized and raging: *I seem sometimes to myself to have only one strong emotion left, only one true passion, and that's hatred, hatred for the forces that have destroyed so many lives, including mine.* I was resigned to the network of outraged recriminations that would entirely entangle him, in which he would thrash and rage until the waters went wine-red with his blood. I was wearily resigned, so that when he suddenly changed direction I was astonished.

— *My own father couldn't have cared less about science.*

The flush of our day's success still on him, he veered suddenly off course. He had gone queerly loquacious, but this was a revelation of an altogether different ordinality, and I felt the deep cold excitement I feel when I am coming into some new knowledge, a sort of icy bliss, it carries me away beyond myself, for I am always, always, a thing that would know.

— *What did he do, your father?*

— *He was a shop owner, sold used furniture in Scranton, Pennsylvania. A very practical man, so of course he thought my kind of science, that didn't lead to any sort of product you could sell, no "better ideas for better living," was a big waste of time. All his cronies at the downtown synagogue had sons who were on their way to making their fathers proud. That was an ongoing theme. I used to promise him that no practical result would ever come from anything I ever did in my life. "That's one of my major goals in life, Pop," I'd tell him.*

The sound of his exceptionally mirthless laugh hung between us for a few bare seconds, a laughter dense with gall.

— *My brother-in-law, my kid sister's husband, Mel Bisseldorf, took over the shop after my father had his first heart attack, and somehow or other Mel became a macher, a millionaire. I never got the details straight.*

— At least you kept your promise to your father.

He glanced over at me and seemed, perhaps, one could never be certain, especially not in this darkening hour, but he seemed, perhaps, to smile.

— My uselessness, you mean? I guess neither of us ever had any doubt about that. "Aside from science," he'd say, "you're a good-for-nuttin'. A big waste of a talent that God must have had something in mind when he chose to give it to you."

Mallach had spoken his father's words with some sort of accent, gesticulating with his hands, his equivocal laughter disappearing into the air, and I was deep in that state of icy bliss, to be allowed this knowledge of the hidden variables of his life.

— He was proud, though, when I got the job here. This place managed to impress him. He came from Europe, you know. Some little town somewhere in Lithuania. He kept all the old ways.

Like my own grandparents, I thought it then and I think it now. My mother's parents lived in Syracuse, New York, not far from Olympia, though I had never set eyes on them nor they on me. I never knew what had inclined them to either Syracuse or to the lilting Anglo tones of my mother's given name. Cynthia. They were not broad-minded in their outlook. Apparent fanatics, they had disowned their studious middle daughter for marrying out of the tribe, breaking her heart just at the point when it was opening up to the world. There was a sort of crazy crisscross here between Dana's forebears and mine, her father Jewish like my mother, her mother Anglo-Irish as my father had been. I thought it then and think it now.

— Still, he was pretty impressed with this place. He thought it was pretty grand.

— *So he saw it, then?*

— *Yes, he saw it.*

Mallach did not think, I do not think, of the difference here between us. It did not cross his mind that my father had not lived to see me set amid the grandeur of this place, a far loftier seat of learning than Olympia College, where he had instructed a handful of undergraduates on the stringent limits of the sayable.

We circled the pond several more times, until he stopped, abruptly, as if he walked alone, turning his melancholy face outward to the pond, so that I watched him in his profile, the long aristocratic arc of his nose and his turned-down lips. Viewed from the oblique angle, the dolefulness he emanated seemed less transcendentally tragic, more supercilious and small. One did not see the contents of his eyes, and he was left looking more acidic and less philosophic. *The world has disappointed me*, this was the message every aspect of him transmitted.

— *I'll tell you something quite interesting about Schrö-dinger. Women were of the utmost importance to his scientific work. There were women — a lot of them — lurking behind his scientific breakthroughs.*

His eyes were fixed straight ahead, and he spoke so low he might have been alone, casting his strange sentences onto the frozen waves of water and air.

— *All of his most important work was done in the midst of passionate love affairs. They fueled his genius. Have you ever heard of Tantrism?*

I started, though I don't think that he saw, his eyes not on me, and I could feel my face take to fire in the cold.

— *A little.*

Briefly, he turned his head and seemed to peer at me.

— You've seen Carlotta's books, then?

I nodded my head beside him.

— A beautiful doctrine, isn't it? Strange and beautiful and infinitely profound.

Dana had spoken similarly. A religious text, she had told me, pulling a volume from Dotty's sacred shelf, an esoteric Hindu work. So that I had been altogether unprepared for what would greet my eyes as she opened its pages.

Garishly colored couples, as well as larger congregations, engaged in every variety of copulation, femininity opening itself to receive immensities of maleness, configurations and entanglements of every conceivable permutation, all versions and perversions and all limned with a detail that seemed more prurient than hieratic, and I had shaken my head in wonder as the little scraps of illegible writing had come tumbling out from between the pages, covered densely with the dead woman's faded scrawlings.

The expressions on the drawn figures had been as strange as everything else, smirking unpleasantly for all the gnostic enlightenment they were claimed to be receiving.

Dana had taken exception to my characterizing the expressions as smirks, telling me their faces had been made strange by ecstasy. *Strange by ecstasy*, she had repeated, rather sternly, though whether it was the mock severity that she sometimes assumed on my behalf I couldn't precisely determine.

— They're scientists of ecstasy, scientists like us.

She spoke it in her most categorical tone of voice, as if she truly meant it, and I searched her face, amused, aroused and appalled by the dark spill of religion that ran through the family, the pious irrationality that seemed to stain them all.

— The Tantra identifies eros, or kundalini, as the source of all creation, in the cosmos as well as in the mind and spirit

and body of man and woman. It's feminine erotic energy, the energy of the goddess Shakti, consort of mighty Shiva.

He paused for some time, and I might have ventured a question, more than several presenting themselves quite readily, but I felt a lurching queasiness in hearing him rave, and kept my silence firm in the hopes that he might do the same.

— *Woman is the sacred fire. The word "cunt" derives from the same source as "kundalini." In Hebrew, we would say they have the same "shoresh," the same root: "cunt" and "kundalini." Did you know that?*

No, I couldn't honestly say that I did, and I shook my head dutifully, my eyes cast downward at the trampled snow. Mallach spoke his revelations in much the same manner in which he had explained to me how naïve realism in regard to quantum operators leads to some of the seeming quantum paradoxes, his voice's ashy languor giving way to bright tints and hard thrusts of emphasis, quickening in his excitement so that he spoke at almost a normal rate and volume.

— *"Cunt" ought to be one of the most sacred words in the vocabulary. That's why we feel such a deep atavistic revulsion when we hear it used as an obscenity. It's a desecration of something fundamental and holy.*

Mallach stared out onto the pond and not at me, as was his style in his own classes, where the students, when their amusement at his antics wore off, could get up and wander out with small probability that the professor would notice their departure. I had heard the rumor, snickeringly related, that he had more than once completed the hour of his lecture in such a state of self-exaltation that there was not a single poet manqué left sitting in the room.

— *All the impetus to break out of the cold comforts of the known, the half-life of normal life, accepting the givens that authority doles out to us — how to live, how to love, how to think — all the energy is drawn up out of the sublime feminine fire of kundalini. The very energy that fuels the cosmos lies coiled deep inside each of us, the potential energy for our salvation.*

I thought to ask him how he meant such terms as "potential energy," whether as a physicist or a poet. But he was in his raving mode, and I declined to enter in.

— Tantric rituals are all directed toward awakening the kundalini. It lies coiled like a serpent at the base of the spine, in the muladhara chakra, in the area called the perineum, and Tantrism teaches techniques for arousing it and drawing it up, through all the seven chakras of the body, so that it becomes gathered into the crown of the skull, in the sahasrara chakra. When this happens, a soul reaches the end of the gnostic journey in a blaze of bliss, matter returning to its source in spirit. It can take a lifetime and it can be very dangerous. Every ecstatic movement of the kundalini carries grave risks. The raising of the fire makes us take risks, you see, and it makes their taking as wonderful as they are terrible. Schrödinger had a very great interest in the philosophy of Tantrism, as did my wife.

And why not? Zen and numerology, palm reading and automatic writing, electromagnetic diets and dialogues with the dead. Why not Tantrism as well? The power of a stupid woman to stupefy a man has a transformative energy all its own, perhaps one and the same with Mallach's kundalini genie.

The path can be very dangerous, Mallach had said, and I could only silently assent. Beside me stood the final product of gnostic burnout, gazing out from his impenetrable sorrow, his lips still moving, as also sometimes happened in his classroom, either because he had momentarily forgotten the existence of his students or because there were segments of his lectures that they were strictly forbidden to hear.

He spoke aloud again, to me, perhaps, I thought it might be to me, though he seemed indifferent to my presence, never glancing at me as he spoke, only out onto the darkening of the little frozen pond.

— *The entire structure of wave mechanics all poured out from a secret tryst of Schrödinger's. He had many known lovers, but the identity of this particular woman has never been learned. He went off with her over the Christmas holidays of 1925 to a little hotel that was also a sanitarium, high in the Swiss Alps, his own magic mountain, and by late January he had already sent off to the* Annalen *the first paper of "Quantization as an Eigenvalue Problem." By February 23,* Annalen *received the second paper, introducing a wave function, psi, as a function in configuration space, and the third and the fourth papers both came soon after. It was a period of sustained creative activity without a parallel in the history of science, and he did it all by himself, like Einstein and relativity, without any collaborators, with the sole exception of whoever that unknown woman was. Schrödinger had a wife, but she wasn't the center of his creative being. For me, it was different. My wife was an extraordinary woman.*

He said this softly and then began to declaim, in the tremulously stilted voice he reserved for his poets, a poem that she and I had read together in Dotty's book, printed out there in the shape of a snake. It always made me cringe with shame for him, the silly falsetto with which he enunciated the verses that he had committed to his diseased faculty of recollection.

— Like a cobra which has cast its coils
           spiralling conch-like three-times-
                      and-a-half round Shiva, her mouth
                   laid on that other mouth
           which leads to bliss,
       the enchantress
   of the world,
       slender as a lotus stem,
              bright as a lightning-flash,
                         lies sleeping,
          breathing softly out and in,
     murmuring poems
            in sweetest meters,
                humming like a drunken bee
                        in the petals of
                    the muladhara lotus,
        how brightly her light shines!

I did not know whether to laugh or cry, to hear him pouring his solemn nonsense into the fallen darkness of that hour. I could not see his face clearly, his eyes and mouth, but I knew the expression of them, the awful outpouring of emotion that matched the excruciating tremolo of his voice.

I did not laugh, I did not cry, and did not grasp at all what it was that Samuel Mallach was trying to tell me in the closing moments of the winter-lit day, talking on and on about things that seemed so irrelevant to our work, and in a manner that left me in doubt as to whether he was even speaking, in fact, to me.

— You owe your scientific ideas to her! But she wasn't a physicist. She didn't know any science.

I finally brought myself to protest the assertion of a Dotty transcendent.

— No, Justin, you misunderstand, you misunderstand me.

It was in my life with her, in its intensity. That's what made it possible for me to think as I did in those days. I will never be able to think with the same intensity again. It was Carlotta who made it possible, who drew the kundalini up into the crown of my skull.

He ended on such a note of forlorn longing, the last inanities sobbing insanely in the frigid air, that I could easily have laughed out loud. He turned at last to face me, and looked at me so searchingly and long that I wondered what he hoped to locate in my face. His gaze had bent itself into an agony of stare, and I suffered its probe with growing discomfort, for it was the gaze of a lunatic or lover: no one elsewise stares like that. What did he want from me, this madman, what did he hope to locate in my face?

I searched the eyes that were searching mine and, all at once, it was with a knowledge that came all at once, one violent flare and then I knew.

He meant to get the glorious physics out from me. That is what he meant. He saw that it was in me and must be aroused so that there was no containing it, the gnostic fire, coiled in some base cranny of my lower body, that it must be heated by applications of sublimity to such a frenzied pitch that it would be forced out from my muladhara chakra, rising upward until it flooded the recesses of my singular skull.

He meant to get the glorious physics out from me and had given me the gift of his extraordinary daughter, as slender as a lotus stem, enchantress of the world, so that it might be done.

I knew it in a moment's span, the merest second's fracturing open, suffered the knowledge as one suffers a blow.

And then something more followed upon this, as effect will follow cause: a further epistemic thrust that was another order of astonishment. It was not like any knowledge I had ever known, but more like a submerged motion in some stratum deeper down than any that I had known to be in me at all.

Like an anchor embedded in the silts of time, it shuddered, and, shuddering, began slowly to ascend, and I could judge all that had lain atop of it only by all the tearing its slow rising did, the slow bulk of it ascending, to squeeze the chambers of my heart, for it was a dreadful ascent, the rising up of my love for him, for Samuel Mallach.

For if there were fathers in science, then there were also sons, and I was his, I felt the great mass of it ascending, that I was his.

The winter's day had given way to night, the properties of darkness more real now than the light, and in that hour he had spoken to me as if unaware of my presence, so that I had not known whether he spoke really to me at all, when he spoke of Einstein, Schrödinger and Dotty, while all the time he was telling me that I was his son and that I was loved.

He stared at me still and he saw, I think he saw, what that dreadful ascent had wrought inside of me, my knowing of his love for me and mine for him, the alteration it had wrought.

She has stolen it from me.

IX

— Leave me alone, Justin Childs!

It makes one smile to see a child's hand scrawl its way across the features of that face, unforming all its beauty, so bloodless now and glazed, even her lips gone waxy white with dread.

— *Justin Childs, leave me in peace!*

X

— My heart is bad.

He answered me plainly, evincing no surprise at all that I should ask my question.

— *That, at least, is what I have been told. That my heart is bad and that eggs and excitement are strictly forbidden.*

— *Is it very serious?*

— *Well, it's pretty serious for me.*

Again there were information-laden looks flowing superluminally between them and excluding me. Had I only dreamed the tenderness of the night before, dreamed a different Dana who had suddenly emerged and taken me in?

I sat across the table from her, her face in profile as she looked sidewise toward her father, his plate of meticulously destroyed toast pushed away from him.

Had her beauty been diminished in my eyes? No. She was still a pharaoh's daughter, though she knew, astonishingly, something of the pharaoh's own science. I wanted to know how much she knew, for in the answer I would know what manner of person she was.

— *My daughter hasn't formally studied a great deal of science.*

I was startled that an answer should come before I had even voiced the question, as if there were improbable waves of influence propagating between the two of us as well.

— *But she knows something about physics? She can understand us when we talk?*

The possibility still amazed me. She didn't look like a person who could understand us. Or did she? Had I looked at her entirely in the wrong light?

— *I thought you weren't real.*

— *Not real?*

— *I thought you were a painting.*

I turned to study her again. She looked annoyed. She had

turned her head so she was staring away from both her father and from me. She took in her breath with slow and audible exaggeration and looked exasperated, her mouth flattened out unpleasantly, turned downward at the ends. Undeniably, I would have said, she looked put out.

— *What do you say to that, Dana? Can you understand Justin and me when we talk? Shall we speak to you more slowly?*

He spoke it out very slowly, as to a little child.

She did not even turn her head to acknowledge him as he spoke. I had thought she doted on his every word. I had thought she was a doter. A fairy girl who would turn to me and speak, an answering angel.

And even so I did not understand her, as I soon would, did not comprehend yet that she was proud of her mind as other women are proud of their home, or of their children, or of their men.

— *Is the quality of my intelligence to be the topic of the day, then?*

Her father laughed. This time I was all but certain it was a laugh.

— *You've offended her, Justin. I'm afraid you've offended her deeply.*

— *I didn't mean to. I'm very sorry. It's just that I never thought . . .*

— *That a girl like me could think? I'm an only child, you know. The genes had nowhere else to go. God had to violate the laws of his own nature and create a girl capable of thought.*

She seemed quite awful then. They both seemed awful. Her father made the noise that was his laugh and she smiled at him, proud to have made him laugh, perhaps, or pleased to have me laughed at. She was a proud girl and verifiably awful, both of them awful, sealed up together inside their closed knowledge, the waves of thought they jointly shared.

— *She studied a little physics at a girls' college that she went to.*

— *Vassar, Daddy. The college was Vassar.*

— *Vassar, yes. How long were you there altogether?*

— *Two years.*

— *Two years. Then you left Vassar in order to marry. . . .*

He trailed off into his strange laughter, and I thought he was making some sort of odd joke, perhaps teasing her for being an old maid, though she was not much older than I. Still, perhaps he thought she ought to have been married by now. Perhaps girls of her age ought to be married.

He turned to me with a self-deprecatory shrug.

— *I always forget the precise name of her former husband. He has one of those perfectly symmetrical names, completely reversible, and I can't for the life of me remember the order. Was it Nathan Martin or Martin Nathan?*

— *Nathan Martin, the physicist?*

— *Yes, Professor Childs. Nathan Martin, the physicist. Oh, of course, you would have known him out in Paradise. Of course. Nathan Martin and not Martin Nathan.*

He gave his strangled chuckle and I stared at Dana Mallach, who was Mrs. Nathan Martin, who was Zeno's quantum muse.

Mrs. Nathan Martin. I might have seen her, then, in Paradise, perhaps pedaling slowly by on her bicycle. I stared at her so intently that she was forced to look at me.

— *Never marry a man who takes Bohr's side in the Einstein-Bohr debate on quantum mechanics. That's my motto.*

She smiled grimly, then stabbed a bit of her egg and brought it to her mouth. The long silence that followed was finally broken by her father, repeating his curious morning greeting.

— *I've been thinking about quantum nonlocality.*

— *So have I, Daddy. What about you, Justin? What have you been thinking about?*

Carefully, I laid down my fork and left the room.

XI

"One of the premier pieces of property in the entire township."

She said this at the front door.

"Imposing and magnificent."

This in the foyer, staring up at the swirling marble stairway.

"Understated elegance. Baronial."

This in the master bedroom, flinging wide the door that Dana would nightly open with tormented care, inches measured out in time, in units of child-terror.

"Oh, just look at the light! What a wonderful addition this room is. The light just pours in and changes the entire feel of it all. Oh, this room is just full of possibilities." So she approves of Dotty's home improvement, the sunroom where the three of us would work, its back wall broken open to transparency.

Back in the imposing and magnificent entrance hall, the woman delicately broaches the subject of an exclusive commission, to which Dana immediately accedes.

"I believe we can set our sights very high. With the market being what it is, and with this location and this house being what they are, I believe we can go very high indeed."

"What is most important to me is that it be sold quickly."

"Yes, I quite understand," though, of course, she doesn't. "I think I can assure you that that won't present a problem. Lord, this property hasn't been on the market for at least the fifty years that Wyndham Realty has existed. How long *has* it been in your family, Dana?"

"I believe my maternal grandparents moved here as newlyweds, but I'm not certain of the year, Miss Wyndham."

"Well, that can easily be ascertained. Just leave it all to me, Miss Mallach."

So Miss Wyndham expertly amends her error. She is no impervious soul, after all, despite the steely glint of the mercantile instinct that she has inherited along with the business.

The little pitch for the virtues of a Wyndham exclusive had been persuasive but not unseemly. Like the baronial master bedroom itself, she gives the impression of an understated elegance; a pale blond and slender woman, perhaps forty-five or more, it is quite impossible with such women to tell; an older version of the tanned fairy princesses who had been so plentiful in Paradise.

"Just so long as you understand, Miss Wyndham, that my overwhelming desire is to get rid of this house as quickly as possible."

There is a something in the tone of the homeowner that makes the heiress of Wyndham Realty stare harder than those of her kind are given to stare. For just a moment, there is a shift in the spread of possibilities in configuration space. The relationship between these two could change quite fundamentally in this moment.

Miss Wyndham laughs. It is a disappointing laugh, a charmschool laugh, and the moment is gone.

"Rid of it? This magnificent piece of property? Miss Mallach, we can set our sights quite a bit higher than that."

What has happened to our high sights now, Mara Wyndham? The opposite of a plain truth, Niels Bohr liked to repeat, is a plain falsehood, but the opposite of a deep truth is another deep truth. This is an aspect of the doctrine of complementarity which Bohr had offered up at every conceivable opportunity, as a response to every quantum question that went beyond the straightforwardly technical. As a hypothesis about physical reality, Bohr's doctrine of complementarity is perhaps not very illuminating, but it may have some value in approaching the complexities of psychological and moral reality, as well as the reality of real estate. For if it is a deep truth of realty that a vacant house is harder to sell than an occupied house, it is just as true that the occupied house on Bagatelle Road has proved impossible to get rid of.

Oddly, Miss Wyndham never comes any more to show it, and she herself must find it odd. Or perhaps she does not. For she has shown herself to be not an altogether impervious soul, Miss Wyndham.

She has shown herself to be quite touchingly susceptible to the appearance of the impossible.

XII

He hovered out of their sight, trying to catch hold of their words.

Mallach's voice came out as an indistinct blur, and his daughter's was barely more intelligible.

They had spoken in such a way as to be understood by one another but not by him. Even a child would have known their behavior to be rude. They had intentionally excluded him and then gloated upon his exclusion.

That was how it seemed to him when he put down his fork and left the room. But before he even reached the doorway, he wondered whether he had been mistaken. They had been submitting him to something or other, but it might, after all, have been a test rather than a taunt. There was something in their voices that had suggested it was a test, a difficult test but nonetheless fair, which meant that there had existed, in theory, the possibility of his comprehending what was going on.

He had always been good at exams. Exams came with the guarantee that all the questions had discovered solutions, and so long as he knew this, he could count on his own brain. He might have passed this one, if only he had realized in time that it was a test. He hadn't, and he had laid down his fork and left the room.

But no, the test could not possibly have been fair. There was no way in the world that he could have figured out what they both knew: that she was Mrs. Nathan Martin. He felt the fact of his unknowing as something terrible. What was terrible was not the fact of who she was, but rather his not having known.

Now everything that was true of her had been rendered a potential torment. It was intolerable what lay hidden inside another, intolerable that you could not divide one person into another with no remainder.

He hovered now outside their sight, outside the dining room doorway in the great marble entrance, a shaft of hard morning sunshine prodding his eyes, and he strained to catch the drift of their conversation, to observe without disturbing.

Mallach's voice was barely intelligible to Justin. Under even the best of circumstances, Mallach was a mumbler. Justin could not make out any of his words at all, and Mrs. Nathan Martin's were hardly more intelligible. Neither Mallach had a voice that was made for easy listening.

"Ergodic," he thought he heard the daughter say. "Ergodic motion."

Why? Why would they suddenly be speaking about ergodic motion, the sort of motion that achieves all possibilities over the course of time?

"Ergodic motion" is what he thought he had heard.

Perhaps she had been using the phrase metaphorically, they were so fond of poetry, those two, the sly stratagems of poetry, its maliciously tortuous deformations of meaning.

Justin strained harder to penetrate Dana's maddeningly muffled voice. She had a strange voice, it was a deep and low voice, that came out of her throat, and with something like a hiss sometimes suppressed in it.

Ergodic motion, he heard it again.

Or had he? Had it been rather *erotic motion*? Or maybe *erotic emotion* or *ergodic emotion*? What had she said?

He was skulking outside the dining room door, dressed in the same clothes he had worn last night to dinner, and he did not know whether the two of them were speaking of matters ergodic or erotic. He had put down his breakfast fork, still skewering the eggs set down by the disquieting Dora, and fled the room, to hide himself out here and eavesdrop, desperate to observe without disturbing, to ascertain the system of which he was a part, he thought he was a part. He had expected that they would speak of him.

"Why quantum?" he thought he heard Dana ask.

Why quantum? or *Why want him?* He was not at all certain. Damn their vocal inadequacies and the dense web of intimacy woven over their private expressions, both spoken and unvoiced.

Had it been *want him* or *quantum?*

"That's the problem we have to solve," he heard her say almost clearly. "That's the problem for us." And then she had laughed, her laughter barely merrier than her father's. Justin could make out its import no better than he had been able to grasp the permutating syllables that had slid themselves past him. Was it awful laughter, as awful as she quite possibly was, though he could not be entirely sure, perhaps she was not awful at all? Was she as awful as he could possibly imagine, and even more than he could imagine?

He saw Zeno, quite suddenly, saw him clearly and distinctly, though it wasn't Zeno in his most characteristic Zeno-esque mode: pacing back and forth rapidly, executing sharp little turns just before he crashed into the wall of their Spartan dorm room, firing off comments, his index finger, the nail bitten painfully down, irregularly punctuating the air for added emphasis.

He saw Zeno instead prostrate on his little bed, his eyeglasses off so that his eyes, cast fixedly on the acoustic-tile ceiling, held an exposed and vaguely sick suggestion.

Unlike Justin and most others, Zeno had been small enough, even stretched out to his fullest, to fit comfortably in the little bed that came with the room. There was still ample space for him and his dirty clothes, and indeed his entire wardrobe was assembled, unwashed, in his bed. For days and days Zeno had inexplicably lain there, dislodging himself only to attend class, because nobody ever missed classes at Paradise Tech, and then returning to his bed, the pile of clothes holding steady. Day after day, he wore the same gray M.I.T. T-shirt and stiffening pair of jeans, crawling out of bed to go to class and crawling back again.

Justin had assumed that dissertational difficulties had suddenly stilled the flying arrow of Zeno, but now the knowledge came into him swiftly that the despondent period of Zeno Wicks had precisely coincided with the abrupt departure from Paradise of Mrs. Nathan Martin. Zeno had spoken to him of his advisor's wife in exactly the same explosively firing locutions in which he spoke of superconductivity and compressed matter, and Justin had never thought to imagine a girl like those who pedaled slowly by, their shining hair kept from obscuring their bright visions of the world with matching headbands.

He tried to remember anything at all that Zeno had said about her, but all that he could recall being told was that Mrs. Nathan Martin was interested in the foundations of quantum mechanics, and that her husband had regarded her interest with mild mirth. He had a good sense of humor, Nathan Martin, many of his bon mots were repeated by graduate students. He liked to say that an interest in foundational matters is a sure sign that a physicist has passed his prime and should be put out to graze in the gentle pastures of scientific dotage. "My wife is prematurely aged," he remembered Zeno having quoted him as saying, though by Justin's calculations, it had been Nathan Martin who had been quite old, at least forty-five, quite possibly more than fifty, certainly too old to have a wife like Mallach's daughter. He kept a young man's body, though, lifting weights and jogging, a young man's way of moving and behaving. Justin hadn't paid close enough attention, but he thought now that there might have been something a little strained in the disparity between Nathan Martin's real and apparent age. He lectured in close-fitting jeans and sandals, the two top buttons of his shirts invariably undone, but that was California, after all, and Justin hadn't thought very much about it. Considering now, he concluded that it was more than possible that Nathan Martin was very attractive to women and that, in order to perpetuate the quality, he mounted a vigorous effort. His light brown hair cascaded past his ears, and he moved his body as if he were paying close attention, and Justin suddenly felt a panged disdain for the man, sharpened painfully by the fact of Martin's being a physicist of the very first tier.

It had definitely never occurred to Justin to connect the phrase "Mrs. Nathan Martin" to a girl like Dana Mallach. He had formed a hazy image in answer to the name: an old-fashioned woman with gray hair pinned up into a loose bun.

He realized suddenly that he had been picturing Madame Curie.

He saw Dana again as she had been last night, as he remembered her from last night. It seemed to him that it had truly been, though there were nights when he awoke holding some woman who had come into existence while he slept, like Eve come from Adam's rib, formed by the appetite he had been just on the verge of gratifying. But it seemed to him it must have happened, that it was a real event and had really occurred, Dana's body arching above him, trembling like a flame above his own, fierce at one moment, tender at the next, her tenderness had been the most terrible aspect of it all, he did not know if he would emerge from it at all. She had trembled above him and he had laid his mouth on her, in kisses that were the first he had placed on any girl, and he did not know if he would ever again make his way out from the experience of the night from which he'd just awoken.

And still she was as beautiful as before, a pharaoh's daughter, throwing off a different light that propagated imbalance and wild awe wherever it struck.

And, stricken, he thought it might have been the ancient light that was the sight streaming down from the sun god's one eye, so that to be in the light was to be bathed in the very sight of the god.

XIII

— That's probably the best argument you can give for the soul's existence.

She laughed softly as she said this, the expression on her face changing in the silk-darkened light, so that the little girl who had been present just a moment before, asking me her naïve questions, instantaneously vanished.

She turned so that she was lying on her side, facing me, the heartbreaking curve of her outer thigh slightly altering its co-ordinates, and I turned too, our faces inches apart, the smell of her mingling with the yearnings entering the bedroom from the night.

— *I thought your view was that the universe took an impersonal attitude toward us — not one that was downright malicious.*

— *Mmm. I waver between cold indifference and low-down malice.*

She smiled, her lips still slightly bruised, and when I reached out my fingers to touch them again she took my hand and opened her mouth and took my fingers into her.

Enchantress of the world.

I watched her face going strange with ecstasy, with a knowledge in her that I could never match, a hidden existence at whose parameters I couldn't begin to guess.

— *Mrs. Nathan Martin.*

I said it aloud. Her eyes flew open and she stared at me, with a look of violation.

— *Why did you call me that?*

— *It's who you are.*

— *No. It's not who I am.*

— *Who are you, then?*

— *What do you mean?*

— *I don't know. I don't know what I mean.*

— *What is it, Justin?*

— *You were her. You were Mrs. Nathan Martin.*

— *And so?*

I groaned, the only answer I could make.

— *Why does that bother you? What can it possibly have to do with you? It barely has anything to do with me.*

She laughed again, her grim laugh. Even her laughter was a painful bafflement to me.

— *How can that be? Tell me something about it! Tell me something so I'll know!*

And once again she laughed, and grimly.

— *Mmm, what can I tell you? Let's see. My husband had terrible views on the foundations of quantum mechanics.*

— *Dana, please!*

— *What is it, Justin, what?*

Her voice was weary, the slight hiss of it exaggerated.

— *I hate the secrets in you. Why is it that prying anything out of you is harder than proving your father's model Lorentz-invariant?*

She laughed at me, this time with real conviction, and she took my head between her hands with tenderness, it felt so much like tenderness, and I held my breath with the thought that she was going to give me one of her rare sweet kisses, that her mouth was going to search after mine.

— *Don't look at me like that, Justin.*

— *Like what?*

— *There's too much of you showing. Don't do that to yourself, don't do it to me. We don't need to know so much about each other. I don't need or want to know.*

— *But I do. I have to, Dana.*

She shook her head at me, disapprovingly, as if to scold me, but there was a film of tenderness still clinging.

— *I thought you learned something about Proust from your mother. Didn't she teach you that lovers make each*

*other up? Every lover is an artist, every love object a con-
struct of the imagination. You've been making me up all
along.*

I felt at a loss at her words, I felt a loss. Something essential
was being stolen from me, snatched out of me before my
eyes, and a shadow of my hurt must have shown itself. A
softness moved over her face, despite the brutal impact of her
words, their slight hard hiss:

— *It's all right to make me up. You have my consent. You
have my active support.*

And still she held my head between her hands, and still it
felt so much like tenderness. And when she let me go it was
to get up from the bed and walk over to the open bay window,
kneeling on the bench, her arms on the sill so that she was
leaning partly out into the night.

I got up, too, to kneel beside her, listening to the night's
soft breaths.

When she began to speak it was in a very low voice, and she
cast her sentences out the open window, not looking at me,
so that I had the feeling that I was, once again, eavesdropping.

— *I went to hear Nathan lecture when he was visiting
here. Of course you know his reputation. And he is a wonderful lecturer, brilliant and funny and so marvelously alive.
He loves to perform. I'd tried to get my father to come with
me, but of course that was out of the question. Listening to a
man like Nathan Martin is the last thing he'd ever voluntarily do. I asked him something during the questioning period
after the lecture, and Nathan said what a good question it
was, that the exigencies of the moment prevented him from
answering in full, but that he'd like to speak to me at greater
length if that was possible.*

— *He said that publicly?*

— *Mmm, or something like it. It was perfectly appropri-*

ate, however he said it. Nathan knows how to carry off almost anything. Especially in front of an audience. In any case, I went over to speak to him after the crowd around him had dispersed somewhat, and he was quite wonderful, seeming to take me very seriously as a physicist, even though I was only an undergraduate. Of course, that would be a very effective form of flattery, given my particular sort of vanity. Nathan's terrific at locating a person's mortal weakness.

She turned her head to me and smiled slightly. She was mind-proud and she knew it. It was the first indication to me that she herself knew.

— He asked me my name and when I told him, he asked me whether I was any relation to Samuel Mallach. He told me how much he wanted to meet him. He told me what a great physicist my father was.

Her voice went even softer, fading out at the end into silence.

— And you married him for that?

She laughed, her grimness reinstated.

— Well, there's certainly more to the story, but as a précis, I think you've got it right. I married him for that. It made me trust him. I trusted Nathan, immediately and unquestioningly, because he'd praised my father. I fell into an abyss of trust.

— And he betrayed you?

— Oh yes. I think one could accurately say that Nathan betrayed me.

— And did it hurt you? Does it hurt you still?

— Yes. I'm rather sensitive to betrayal.

— Me, too.

— Mmm, you would be. It's especially hard for people like us, who give our trust so rarely. I trust almost nobody. I don't even trust the universe.

— I know. I don't either.

— No. We've neither of us much reason for trusting it. But I do trust my father. I trust him with all my soul, Justin. I love him with all my soul.

We were kneeling naked side by side on the little cushioned bench beneath the window, our arms resting on the sill, leaning forward so that we were suspended half-outside. Her bedroom was in the back of the house, right above the glass-walled room where by day we chased down the properties of light.

We were leaning partly out the window, into the insinuations that were crowding the night, all manner of desires carried weightless in thin air. Beyond the grounds of their home were the woods, filled with deer, and it was toward the woods that we looked. We didn't look at each other.

— I do, too, Dana. I love him, too.

— I know you do, Justin. I know.

XIV

She means to live as small and unobserved as if unbeautiful.

She is beautiful still, a deepened beauty, all but submerged to most sight, the cold disenchantment in her extraordinary eyes, the fatalism limned in her mouth. And then there is the limping branded leg and the hands and arms with their discolorations in the shape of rising flames, and these, too, have cast her out from the golden net of others' dreams.

Do you dream of me, Dana?

If her beauty is ever glimpsed at all, over the years, it is usually by someone of her own gender. A rare expression of concealed spirit will rise suddenly into her features, and a female colleague or some still softly opening undergraduate will be caught amazed in the thought that she is beautiful.

Her beauty is largely lost on the men. The distances she keeps are frozen wastelands. Gazed at from the other side and she is stiff and hard and bloodless, so that men shiver.

— *She's beautiful*, he thought, and then he shivered.

For seven years on seven, she has drifted, from one obscure teaching post to another, from this mediocre college to the next: there are so many.

She is not a well-liked teacher. Her students call her "mean" and "creepy," sometimes even "spooky." At the slightly better schools, where some wit lives, they call her Professor Maladjusted or Dr. Malady. She is always meticulous in the distances she keeps, and there is little sympathy flowing in either direction across the space. Those who don't enter her classes science-phobic become so soon enough.

Even her voice sounds as if it comes from a distant and an unlit land, low without being soft, with that suggestion of a hiss that has grown more pronounced in her solitude.

She wants no pity, though. If you show her pity, she'll freeze you dead.

She works on in her obscurity, limping from place to place and never publishing. Some years ago, she sent some papers out, choosing only the very best journals. She sent four papers out and, some months later, they all came back, churlishly annotated. She read the referees' reports with little outward passion, noting that the same orthodoxy that had frozen her father out was still holding firm.

It was not only the content of her papers that brought down on her such lofty contempt, but her style of expression. More than one of the assigned readers had commented that she did not write like a physicist, and, oddly, hadn't intended their remarks as praise. She still holds fast to the doctrine her father had instilled in her, that the very best physics is very good poetry, so that when she can, she always chooses metaphor over mathematics.

One speaks of the "reality problem" in quantum mechanics and it is simply this: "What is quantum mechanics about?" Is there a "there" out there? Some have been tempted to offer a paraphrase of the Bard as an answer: We are such dreams as stuff is made of. *We present instead a picture, wherein psi — the dream field, as it were — stands on a par with "stuff."*

The referees had been too scornful to take in her results, some of which had been entirely original to her, and had been rigorous and real. They hadn't seen what she'd achieved at all.

She reads their uncomprehending remarks with no detectable reaction, except that for several weeks or months or years, she does no more work on quantum physics, only limping on her way, the departments she visits and the students she teaches barely differentiable to her each from each.

It is a kind of purgatory for her, this cruel trajectory she traces from one mediocre department to the next. It is the perfect purgatory for such a person as she, so mind-proud and so alone.

Her contract up, she flees to yet another in the series of academic outposts, crisscrossing the country, east and west, and north and south.

Like an electron in a cloud chamber, she barely registers at all, and how could one be certain she'd been there? She teaches her courses and then she flees. No students come to speak with her. And even in those remote rural collegiate settlements, where colleagues fiercely bond in incestuous arrangements born of desperation, she is left alone, her need for absolute solitude laid bare.

— *She's beautiful*, he thought, and then he shivered. He was a physicist, quite young, an open, affable soul, one felt it on first contact, so that even she seemed slightly warmed.

— *I'm afraid you'll find the students here indifferent at best. Don't be discouraged. But don't come in with expectations of inspiring them to heights of pure science. They're "uninspirable," if that's a word.*

Something moved in her, so that she smiled slightly and thought to answer in something of her old way.

— *Mmm. I don't know that "inspirable" is even a word.*

— *She's beautiful*, he thought, and then he shivered.

For seven years on seven, we have lived quietly, succeeding in avoiding all notice, living and partly living, limping on in our purgatorial peregrinations.

Until we arrive here.

And how is it, after all, that it is *here* that we finally arrive?

Is it a matter simply of the laws of probability dictating that, covering the field of mediocrity as thoroughly as we do, our passing through *here* is just as likely as our having passed through all those other *theres*? Or is it some more directed influence propagating itself across the space of possibilities?

One would think that I would know, yes, one might think.

There are many towns around these parts named after the heroic past of a dead antiquity: Ithaca, Utica, and Troy; Rome, Syracuse, Corinth, Phoenicia, Attica, Carthage; Homer, Hannibal, Cicero; the mythical memories entangled in the geography of upstate New York.

At first, she goes along in her old ways, barely taking note of those around her, teaching her classes and then vanishing from sight. But slowly, slowly a change is being wrought.

She learns the names of some of her best students.

She has lunch with a colleague in her department and goes for a walk with another, who decelerates his pace to join her limp. One night he takes her out to dinner and the two of them drink wine. He takes a great deal of time deliberating over the bottle, not wanting to err. They read the overwrought characterizations of each vintage together, so many adjectives squandered on squeezed grapes, he quite solemn at first, until she relaxes him with her skepticism, and they pick an unsuitable wine for the sheer absurdity of its descriptive prose.

She learns the names of her worst students and has them come to her office for extra help.

The dinner companion asks her out again, his name is Wallace Low, he is widowed and balding, portly and courtly. His understanding of physics is pedestrian, his jokes quite possibly even worse, but she smiles at all of them and twice I see her laugh.

She learns the names of all her students and I see her laugh aloud in class one day and they all laugh with her.

Has an unnaturally wholesome influence entered the field around her? Or is it a matter rather of a sinister something having been withdrawn, the metaphysical blight diminished? One would think that I might know, yes, one might think.

And little by little it is all coming back: the physics that had burned through the hours of our days and nights, the hours of our lives.

The mysteries of the particles and waves; the gnostic field of knowing that links each to each: all must merge in

Einstein's truth, but who can see it, who see how? There are problematic quantities spinning wildly off to infinities, infinities intruding where they cannot be tolerated, and how might they be subdued and who might see how? Not Einstein himself, who had declared, some years after accomplishing the revelations of his general relativity:

I will devote the remainder of my life to thinking about light.

— I've been thinking.

I despaired in general when she spoke those words, drawing the fire away from the pure forms of math that I knew must someday yield up the sought solution.

— The wave function . . .

— Yes, Dana, what?

— Maybe psi is the mathematical expression for mind.

A light like lunacy had gone on in his eye, and I had wondered yet again how it was that these two could be the scientists they were and yet entertain such thoughts, could believe that mind or spirit might be lurking in the equations, when the properties of matter in motion are the only properties that there are, so I had wondered and so I had erred.

She pulls out the old yellow lined pads of paper she used to hold on her lap while the three of us worked, notebooks filled with her old quantum scribblings, packed up and toted along through all her weary crisscrossing. She stares at the pages of faded equations, the tangle of starry triangles that she had drawn around them.

There is some way of seeing we have not yet seen, a seeing still unsighted in the long corridor of links, and without it even the most powerful mathematics gropes blind.

The deepest truth we have ever known about the substance of light is that it is itself invisible.

So it is that she has come here, to *my* Olympia.

And all things linked are.

XV

— Thou canst not stir a flower without troubling of a star.

In the morning light, she quoted the poetry without blushing the color of the deep night wine, in such a tone and at such a pace as if to get it out of the way.

XVI

"An impossible man."

Justin turned to follow Dietrich Spencer's gaze and caught a glimpse of the flitting figure of Samuel Mallach vanishing around a corner.

It was Indian summer, a late afternoon at the end of September, the autumn semester still new, the distractions of the classroom therefore many. Spencer had detained Justin in the corridor, speaking a few words to him, not in order to inquire after his class enrollments (they were, as always, not high), but to ask him a question relating to their work.

One or another of the senior physicists was always summoning Justin to bring the fire of mathematics down to them. He didn't resent their requests. Dana resented them, but he didn't. He was the most junior of the faculty members at a most important place, and he was in no position to balk at the attention of any senior faculty member, least of all Dietrich Spencer's.

Spencer often asked Justin to come round to his office, in the late afternoon, after the daily departmental tea. In his first few months, Justin had rarely attended these events, but under the persuasions of Spencer, who placed great emphasis on the camaraderie of the teas, he had begun to frequent them quite regularly, as well as the various departmental meetings and even some more sociable events.

There was no doubt that the powerful figure of Dietrich Spencer had taken a shine to Justin Childs. From the very beginning Spencer had seemed to like him, unaccountably, for he was not so very likable and Spencer was not so inclined to like. He held his explosive impatience noticeably in check when dealing with Justin Childs, and had assigned Justin an office in seventh heaven, a small office not far from his own.

Justin's doctoral dissertation advisor had been Helmut Zweifel, and Zweifel and Spencer had been collaborators, years ago, on background radiation, the work that was still awaiting the summons from Stockholm. It must have been Zweifel's letter of recommendation on behalf of Justin Childs that had swayed Spencer so decisively — Spencer himself had hinted broadly that this was so, that candidates more conspicuously dazzling had presented themselves for the department's favor. Some other senior members of the department, each pushing for his own choice, had opposed Childs's appointment with special vigor — this, too, Spencer had indirectly let Justin know — swooping down on what they read as the damning praise bestowed in Helmut Zweifel's letter. Zweifel had extolled the candidate as a demonstrably gifted mathematician, but, on the matter of his talents as a physicist, had resorted to a set of refined equivocations. Justin unearthed the letter, at one of those hours when he had the corridors almost entirely to himself, coming only, once or twice, upon a deeply distracted, deeply disbelieving graduate student or very junior faculty member.

As a physicist, Justin Childs is, without a doubt, the best mathematician I have ever met. . . . Since coming to California, I have become quite a Lakers fan, and, in summary, my assessment of Justin Childs can be expressed in the terms of their game. Justin Childs is a genius of sorts, a genius at assist. He will not necessarily get the ball into the hoop, but it is a likelihood bordering on certainty that he will pass the ball to the one who will score.

Spencer's colleagues must have pecked at Zweifel's niceties, but Spencer would have prevailed, as was his wont. He often spoke, with a disingenuous show of wonder, of the "hidden hand" that mysteriously conduced to total unanimity in most departmental decisions, and when Justin arrived he found a chairman ready to take him under a forceful wing.

Dietrich Spencer could be almost overwhelmingly charming, as Justin, charily uncharmed, had often observed, sensing an insidious intent in the methodically affable urbanity.

Spencer reveled in the *ex cathedra* graciousness he showed important visitors, always taking it upon himself to introduce them with full ceremony, describing their work with such freehanded application of superlatives that the very few who felt the lavishments undeserved nervously wondered whether they were being ridiculed. Justin watched closely, finding Spencer always instructive if not reassuring.

Still, if only through the dulling effect of familiarity, Justin's disquiet in the presence of Dietrich Spencer had been subdued to a level almost imperceptible to both. Justin had largely gotten over his edgy awareness of the man's stored-up reserves of energy, his unnerving voice and more than unnerving scar — all the signs that pointed obliquely to the something brutal that was being held in check. Justin barely even noticed now the left fingers snapping.

At first the scar had drawn his attention irresistibly, so that Spencer had noticed him trying not to take note.

"You are no doubt wondering how I got this elaborate decoration."

Spencer had pointed to the mutilated strip on his brow and smiled paradoxically, his eyebrows arched ironically but his mouth almost gleefully turned up.

Justin, trapped like a child, didn't know what to say, whether to deny it or confess, but Spencer continued on, with customary gusto, as if he quite enjoyed to speak of the sinister-looking flaw.

"A memento of a fight from long ago, when I was a hotheaded youth, with quixotic views of honor and heroism. It's a frightful thing, I know, quite Frankensteinian. But you should see what the other fellow got."

And he laughed, the powerful gaze of his grayish blue eyes distressingly ablaze, while Justin remembered the story he had heard of a Heidelberg duel. It occurred to him to wonder whether the "other fellow" had perhaps been left dead.

"An impossible man."

Spencer said it in a low voice, almost beneath his breath, his left hand snapping, and Justin turned to follow the trajectory of the vanishing physicist, and then turned back again to stare at Spencer.

By tacit consent, neither Justin nor Mallach ever gave away any sign that they were more than distant colleagues. When Justin spoke to Spencer of his other research, he did not mention Mallach's name, nor Mallach's model, nor anything immediately or derivatively Mallachian.

Justin knew his reasons for his obliquity, and so must Mallach have known his own.

"One could make the case that the department's loyalty to its own exceeds itself in the case of Samuel Mallach. The man's a loon."

It was a vulgar expression and very much out of Spencer's public character, which observed a rigorously systematic courtesy. It was only in isolated episodes that he lost his temper and the contained ferocity escaped, most usually to the detriment of his two secretaries, Della and Joyce. Neither was young — Della, in fact, his "personal assistant," had worked for him for almost twenty-five years — but both had a girlish quality that rose to the surface in the presence of their boss. With other members of the department they could be brusque and blunt and bossy: in the case of Della, very bossy. She had even acquired the habit of snapping her fingers, though not so deathly softly as he. Della and Joyce behaved as if they regarded the majority of the faculty as little more than difficult children requiring a very firm hand. But

Dr. Spencer utterly drained the firmness out of them both, they went as floppy as rag dolls, and it was discomfiting to see the effects on them of his unloosed rage.

"He's a loon," he repeated, his voice not bothering to disguise his contempt, so that Justin's lulled terror reawakened and gave a little yelping leap.

Still, Spencer's reasons for the denunciation seemed fairly obvious to Justin. As chairman of the celebrated department, in which he took an understandable pride, he was naturally vexed at having to retain the burnt-out, if tenured, figure of Samuel Mallach. Nobody in the department, least of all the impatiently dismissive Spencer, would ever have entertained the possibility that there was still some serious science to be gotten out of the relic assigned to teaching Physics for Poets.

And yet the work at Bagatelle Road had been creeping steadily forward, at a laboriously slow rate, for there was a great deal of unbroken-in mathematics to tame into place, but nonetheless they were steadily creeping forward and toward the light.

Mallach's office at the top of the stairs was too cramped for the three of them to occupy, so they had moved themselves into the sunny room at the back of the house. Sometimes the deer from the woods just beyond their property would come. Mallach and his daughter put out fruit to draw them near. The two were always watching for the soft, trembling approach. It was yet one more large distraction with which Justin was forced to contend. One or the other would point, and all three would turn to gaze. Justin liked to watch the animals, too, though it was Samuel Mallach who truly loved them, and Dana loved them for her father's sake.

They used a child's chalkboard to sketch out their calculations. There were still days when Mallach balked at the hidden physics that lay before them, the cruelly twisted skeins of mathematics that they had yet to unwind.

"Quantum problems are like kabbalah," Mallach said. "They're dangerous. They drive men mad."

On such days he would agree to nothing but to listen to his daughter read from his chosen poets.

> *Then tell me, what is the material world, and is it dead?*
> *He laughing answer'd: I will write a book on leaves*
>   *of flowers,*
> *If you will feed me on love-thoughts, and give me now*
>   *and then*
> *A cup of sparkling poetic fancies; so when I am tipsie*
> *I'll sing to you to this soft lute, and show you all alive*
> *The world, when every particle of dust breathes forth*
>   *its joy.*

This was Blake. This he knew.

Study Blake, he had admonished Justin; study Yeats. But there was more than Blake and Yeats for Justin Childs to study now.

They had composed a thought-picture and it was beautiful. They needed only to know whether it was also true. But now they had a picture of time working its way out in quantum gravity, and if they could only work out the math, as time itself works its way out, then they might begin to believe in their thought-picture and begin to make it known.

Justin had gone from studying the songs of Blake, to studying first-order diffeomorphism-invariant dynamics, the mathematics he was convinced would yield up the final reckoning.

At first he had worked on the forms on the sly, fearing the Mallachian reaction. But on an afternoon in the dead of winter, a few days after they had celebrated Christmas quietly together, he had gotten them to see how his fire could be fused to their intuitions, and they had begun, at their different rates, to take the fire into themselves.

For Samuel Mallach it was a cold struggle to assimilate the new math, but Dana was warming quickly to the structures that Justin urged on her. The math was not yet as beautiful as the two of them knew it would be. It was still a twisted skein and it was rough. If they could work it out so that it was beautiful, so that it was diaphanous and lit, then they would know. And then they would tell the world.

Compared to the work they were pursuing in the house on Bagatelle Road, Spencer's requests were child's play.

Spencer regained himself quickly, after the interruption that Mallach's flitting passage had presented, and took up again the broken thread of his thought.

"I must leave tomorrow for that conference at Berkeley. It would be convenient for me to be able to have the solution before my talk. It will make for a more interesting lecture!"

Spencer laughed, opening his mouth wide, and Justin, taller by quite a bit, saw a few gold teeth gleaming at the back. The sight of this gold was also vaguely unsettling to him. It looked European and recalled sinister stories. He knew he was staring too bluntly into Spencer's mouth. He had quite forgotten to laugh at Spencer's wit, to respond at all to Spencer's implicit but imperious summons.

"Let's meet a little later this afternoon, shall we? And then we can work straight through the evening, as long as it takes!" Spencer commanded, snapping his protégé back to attention.

Justin called the Mallach home, to tell them he would not be coming at all today.

"It's Spencer, isn't it? Wanting to pick your brain again," Dana said.

"Yes, it's Spencer."

"The man is frightful."

"Yes, I think you're right."

"I'll have to make up some story to tell my father."

"There seems to be no love lost when it comes to Spencer's attitude toward your father."

"Mmm. Well, there's little love lost on Daddy's side either. He's got a very warm seat in the inferno reserved especially for Dietrich Spencer. I think he's got all the physicists slated for the ninth circle of hell, but he's keeping the central pit reserved exclusively for sexy Dietrich."

"Sexy?"

"Mmm."

Her permutating mmm's served her in many ways, assuming a host of meanings. This one was drawled out, playful and yet effective, and he felt it working on him, uncomfortably, while in addition it made him jealous, the sly implications of her softly laughing *mmm*.

"I think you actually mean that."

"There's a theory that evil is erotic, and the consequence of that would be that Dietrich Spencer is sexy as all hell. To hear my father speak, the history of that one man duplicates the entire history of all the atrocities of twentieth-century physics."

"Does that include Hiroshima and Nagasaki?"

"Mmm. You raise an interesting question. Personally, I think my father suspects that Dietrich was working for the Nazis. Which isn't so inordinately unlikely. There's that first name and the unidentifiable accent that seems to wander all over the globe."

"Not unlikely at all. There's that terrible scar."

"There's no crime of which Daddy wouldn't gladly suspect Dietrich capable. Which is all very odd because I seem to remember that when I was a very little girl he was Uncle Dietrich."

"That must have been before your father discovered he was a Nazi spy."

"You'd better watch your step. The man might still be spinning schemes of fascist domination. Like the professor that Orson Welles, also sexy, played in that movie. Nazi or not, I'll have to make up some story for my father. You realize that."

"Do what you think you must."

"I don't like to lie to him, you know. I never used to have to lie to him before."

"What do you want me to do? Say no to Spencer?"

"Say no. Why not?"

"You're unreasonable."

"It's not as if Spencer is even doing important work. The rumor is that even his work on background radiation, which was eons ago, was simply a lucky break. He just stumbled on it in the dark, stubbed his great big lucky toe on it."

"I've actually heard that even when he had stumbled on it, he didn't quite make out its cosmic shape or significance. Someone had to explain the cosmological consequences to him, how it connected up with the big bang. He hadn't realized the implications for himself."

"Really? I never heard that. Who was it?"

"Actually, the name that was mentioned to me was your father's."

He heard nothing at all, not even the quiet intake of her breath.

"Dana?"

"Mmm."

"Just wondering whether you're still with me."

"I am. I just don't know quite what to make of what you just told me."

"Listen, Dana, I have to go now."

"As I must go and lie to my father."

"It's all empty work, what I'm doing with Spencer, child's play."

"Then why go off and work with him? Our work isn't empty child's play."

"It's precisely because what Spencer is doing is so insignificant that all this fuss over whether we lie to 'Daddy' or not is so nonsensical. It's of no consequence, Dana. I barely even have to think in order to do what it is Spencer needs."

"I have to go downstairs to him now and concoct a story. That's of consequence."

"Well, if you think that lying to him is so unthinkable, just tell him the truth."

"That's even more unthinkable, Justin, and you know it."

"Dana, are there really nine circles of hell?"

"Precisely. And the ninth one is reserved for traitors, and what Dante saw there was too terrible to be described. *'I did not die, and did not remain alive! Think now for thyself, if thou hast a grain of wit, what I became, deprived of one and the other.'* Does that sound vaguely familiar, Justin?"

"It sounds like Schrödinger's cat paradox."

"Exactly." She chuckled low into the phone. "Wouldn't you know that in the very center of hell you'd find the measurement problem."

XVII

— Tell me, what is the material world, and is it dead?

It is Professor Mallach and the course is "Physics for Poets," an unprecedented success this year.

— In the famous two-slit experiment, both photons and electrons can be made to behave schizophrenically: both like a particle and a wave. But here's something even stranger: the troubled entities only behave psychotically when they're unobserved. The physicist infers the schizophrenic motion from the scattering traces that are left behind on a photographic plate. If someone actually looks at their behavior prior to the final detection, the aberrations vanish, and the electrons and photons conduct themselves like proper particles, unsplit and reassuringly normal.

One might think that the predicaments of quantum mechanics, as bad as they are, can at least be confined to the microscopic level, where we at least don't have to see them. Electrons would then be like those demented family members that used to be kept hidden out of sight in the attic. But as any good student of nineteenth-century fiction knows, you can't keep the mad attic-dwellers of the imagination locked up forever. At some point the whole house burns down. The famous thought experiment known as "Schrödinger's cat paradox" is like Mr. Rochester's wife in Charlotte Brontë's Jane Eyre. *You remember how just before Jane was to marry Mr. Rochester, his very mad wife, Bertha, escaped from her watched keep at the top of the house and set the place on fire, making her hidden existence terribly known? What "Schrödinger's cat" accomplished is something similar for the material world. It shows us that the madness of quantum mechanics can't be conveniently confined on the microscopic level, and this, too, is rather terrible.*

They laugh with her when she wants laughter, and seem to be stirred when she would have them stirred. In class after class, from her Physics for Poets to her more advanced students, they do not pack up to go until she nods that she is done. Can it be they are even learning something of physics?

This they sense: how much she loves. The physics that had burned through the hours of our days and nights, the hours of our lives.

— *The world as it really is, after all, the world as it really is.*

That is how he put it.

— *To turn away from the shadows on the back cave wall, to step out from inside the cave and see the world as it really is, after all.*

He gestured with his hands in motions that were fluid and somehow beautiful. The movements of youth and beauty were preserved in his flowing hands, and her face was caught in some mystery of ardor above the play of candlelight, as she listened to him rhapsodize on the search after truth as a physicist knows it.

It is only a pale reflection of that night's ardor that plays over her face now, but the students catch the flicker of it, or so it seems, and the implication of real passion transfixes them, young as they are and dullish in the myriad ways of inference, they appear to catch the passion's flash, and so it is that they laugh with her when she wants laughter and never pack up their books until the final nod that she is done.

XVIII

"They're scientists of ecstasy, scientists like us."

Justin stared at her, trying to take the measures of her face and voice so that he might judge to what degree to take her seriously.

"'Scientists of ecstasy,' Dana. How shall I understand that?"

"Perhaps by thinking very hard." She spoke it in her grandest tone of voice, her most superior, as if she really meant it, gave credence to possibilities so remote they barely qualified as possibilities at all, and he was amused, appalled and aroused, and all at once. "Mmm." She hummed it deep down in her throat. "It's a lovely word. I'm very taken with the word."

"Scientist?"

She turned her head around on the pillow to face him, and laughed with that thin sharp edge of triumph that sometimes poked through when she thought him a fool.

"Ecstasy, Justin. *Ecstasy."*

"I know." Justin ran a finger across her cheek. "I'm not that much of an idiot."

It was because she thought him such an unredeemable nerd — with some justification — that she was willing to believe in any degree of his obtuseness. Still, she allowed his finger to continue to trace small circles on her cheek and down her neck. She was wearing a soft black sweater that he loved on her, the way it set off the glowing pallor of her skin.

"Aren't you?" she murmured. "I don't know if I'm relieved or not to hear that." She took his finger in her hand and considered it. "Do you know the etymology of the word *ecstasy?"*

"It's from the Latin. It means: to stand beside."

"And what is it that the ecstatic stand beside, o promising youth?"

She had turned his hand over and was inscribing her web of

triangles very lightly across his palm with the very tips of her fingers, which made it a formidable problem for him to think, although he was determined to try.

"Themselves, of course."

"Mmm, so you do know something about ecstasy after all, Justin Childs."

The edge had vanished from her voice. She had gone over to something closer to tenderness, it felt like tenderness to him. They were lying side by side in her little white bed, propped up on a pile of pretty little pillows, and had been studying one of Dotty's erotico-esoteric texts. Samuel Mallach had excused himself to take a nap before dinner, and there was still just enough wintry light to see by, though they had to hold the heavy tome quite near their eyes. Justin's weak eyes were straining through the lenses of his glasses at one of those voluptuously descriptive paintings that had initially shocked him, and that continued secretly to shock him still, and she would laugh at him if she knew.

When he had been a mournful nerd, too alone to have any sense of how lonely he was, wandering through the glare of Paradise grasping his moist dream of someday speaking to a girl, she had been Mrs. Nathan Martin, the wife of a physicist of the very first tier. There was a world of worldly experience that separated them still, an indivisible remainder inside her to torment him.

The book was open to a painting of "a prince and princess of Jodhpur," perched on luxurious cushions and gazing wide-eyed into each other's eyes, palm to palm, and maintaining a highly improbable position.

"They never seem to close their eyes, these Tantric people. Is that part of their religion?"

"Yes, as a matter of fact. The gaze is required. They see the divine in each other. She sees Shiva in him, and he sees Shakti in her. And when they move, it's the gods moving in their limbs."

"Frankly, Dana, it's hard to imagine how they move at all in that particular pose."

The royal lovers were dressed in nothing but elaborate jewelry, flimsy veils and those strange expressions over whose apt characterization Dana and he could come to no agreement. The smirking prince's legs were folded into the open lotus position and his smirking princess sat on his lap, her legs wrapped around him, the precise circumstances of their congress vividly executed.

"That's where you're wrong, Justin. That's where you're grievously in error. There are all sorts of hidden movements going on, movements physical and metaphysical."

"Metaphysical movements." Justin laughed and she smiled back at him with sweet serenity intact, not taking his jeering to her heart, perhaps because she took him altogether so little to her heart. "Now there's an expression to challenge the limits of the meaningful."

"And yet metaphysical movements nonetheless. That's a very advanced position, very conducive to meditation."

She persisted in her sententious tone of voice, and he laughed again, still not able to determine for certain how serious she was.

"And upon what, exactly, would they be meditating in their very advanced position?"

"The same things upon which we meditate in our very advanced science, Justin. The ultimate nature of reality. The shimmering veil between appearance and reality. The smug erroneousness of received opinion."

"Couldn't they meditate better at some further distance from each other?"

"Do you meditate better apart from other scientists?"

"Oh, come off it, Dana. Science is by nature collaborative. I always thought mystical enlightenment was a solitary sort of affair, not to speak of asexual. Some bony guy in a loincloth humming *om* on a desolate mountain."

She allowed herself to smile, the lights breaking out in her eyes.

"I think you're generally quite right. Even Shiva himself was said to fit that description, smeared with ash and arrogant as only a man in a loincloth can be, until his presumptions were blasted by the illuminating ecstasy of the goddess."

"So it was the goddess who enlightened the god."

"Of course. Kundalini is feminine erotic energy. I distinctly remember having explained that to you."

"Of course."

"Of course. This particular position, by the way," she pointed to the Jodhpur pair, "is supposed to be very effective in provoking the kundalini to ascend."

"Moving up through the seven chakras toward the great gnostic orgasm."

"Speaking of orgasms, Justin, Tantric experts are said to have been able to do the most amazing things. They could perform feats of eroticism that almost defy the imagination."

"I tremble to ask."

"As well you should. At the most advanced Tantric level, there are sexual yoga techniques called *mudras*, which means 'seals.' Everything is carried out with infinite slowness, at a rate conducive to meditation. The most advanced of all is called the *amaroli*, or immortal, *mudra*, and it requires the man drawing his released seed back into himself, now that it's been mingled with his lover's essence."

"Sounds revolting, not to speak of unhealthy."

"The idea behind all Tantric sex is to bind the two bodies together into one system of energy, the seven chakras becoming fourteen, with the long loops of released energy swirling through their joined bodies. If they can lose themselves entirely in this, like two ecstatic dancers only conscious of the dance, no longer knowing where one body ends and the other begins, then they have the experience of really being one. And this, Justin, is the instant in which they feel themselves absorbed into the divine."

"No doubt."

This time she allowed herself true laughter, unchecked and childlike.

Justin leaned over her and took her head between his hands. "You don't believe a word of it, do you, Dana? Chakras and kundalini. The gods moving in lovers' limbs or the mind of God lurking in the equations. You don't believe a single silly syllable of it. You're just playing around with all this high-minded hokum. But in the end you're a hardheaded little rationalist, Dana Mallach."

"A rationalist? Don't accuse me of that, Justin Childs. Anything but that." She said it with a great show of feigned horror, then grinned and moved herself closer, sliding herself halfway under him.

"I've seen through to you now. I've torn off the last of the shimmering veils. You're a thoroughgoing little skeptic. You believe in metaphysical motions just about as much as I do."

He was propped up on his elbows over her.

"Well, no, there's a difference between us. I do try and maintain an open mind. Still, the sense of the absurd does tend to invade. I think I do have a certain inherited suscepti-bility to the mystical . . ."

Justin snickered.

"I do, but the sense of the absurd may come out just a bit stronger in me."

"God bless you for your sense of the absurd, Dana. God bless you for it."

"Listen to *you*, summoning the Problematic Entity to bless me for my blasphemy."

She reached for her mother's book, pulling it nearer to them, and tapping a finger on the amorous center, the *svadis-thana chakras*, of the royal couple.

"We might give it a try, Justin, in the sacred spirit of science."

"You think?"

"I do."

"It *would* be worthy of us as scientists."

"Even though we're theoreticians, not experimentalists." She had slid out from under him and, kneeling before him and frowning slightly, was attempting to arrange his long stiff legs into a poor approximation of the lotus position. She herself could fold herself up into the pose with graceful ease. "Still, it would be an impressive application of the hypothetical-deductive method."

"I don't believe I'm familiar with the hypothetical-deductive method. Another Tantric sexual ritual?"

She leaned back on her heels and laughed again, with all her childlike unrestraint, taking her hands off his legs so that they came undone and he lost all pretense of lotushood.

"The hypothetical-deductive method, according to certain philosophers of science with whom Daddy qualifiedly concurs, is supposed to describe what scientists do. You assume a position, one with possibilities enough to deserve attention, and then see what follows." She smiled. "How very well I explained that. How very well that came out."

Justin laughed back at her.

"What's so funny?"

"You're so absurdly proud of your own mind, Dana. You're such a mind-proud girl."

"I've a right to be. It's a good mind. Or can't you appreciate it?"

"I'm brimming over with appreciation: 'You assume a position' " — he pointed to the ecstatically smirking prince and princess of Jodhpur — " 'and then see what follows.' How could I fail to appreciate such a mind?"

How could I have failed?

XIX

Her students and she are dancing out the physics of turbulent flow.

She takes them out onto the fading lawn in the center of the hilltop campus of Olympia College. It is Indian summer, the days luxuriously warm, the weather of sweltering August, even though the trees are raving mad with color, and they hold the complex equations of fluid mechanics inside of them. She tells them how to do it.

In the classroom, the Navier-Stokes equations are chalked up on the board, and now they take them out into the late afternoon, the thick light sifting through the ambers and golds to fall heavily on them, to paint them with its glaze.

She is no longer graceful. There is the limp and there are the years, there is the accumulation of the heavy years. But she feels it still, feels the physics still inside of her, in the movements of her muscles, and she tries to explain it until they can feel it as she does, so that the knowledge she holds within her body will leap like fire into them, into their own bodies.

They move together across the browning lawn in the late-autumn day, their motions choreographed by the Navier-Stokes equations, which are still staring down at the empty classroom from the blackboard. Beside them are words of poetry very faintly traced in chalk:

But one man loved the pilgrim soul in you.

— Now we know it.

She says this to them as they collapse down on the grass around her, the packet of them collapsing, and every last one of them is laughing.

With the light of the late afternoon dripping slowly on the lawn and mixing with their soft, lit laughter, all the tender loveliness of their faces and their laughter laid open in the sorrowing grass, and I think that they must love her, that she is loved. In the late afternoon, her face no longer young, and she is loved.

Her father bade her to recite the poem and so she did, never expecting me to be anything more than the thing that I was, more than Justin Childs, a sad thing to contemplate in the light of the dying fall.

For in the end I was but a nerd, too nerdy by far to care: to see it as a condition of unknowing, for all of the knowing entailed. The word hardly signified to me, reaching me indistinguishable as some far-off phantom choir, as words written out in palest swirls of chalk in an emptied classroom:

> *But one man loved the pilgrim soul in you,*
> *And loved the sorrows of your changing face.*

In the dying fall, her face no longer young, and my Dana, my Dana is loved.

XX

Nobody in the physics faculty common room took note that a singularity had just occurred.

He slipped through the door, entirely undetected, and not a soul glanced his way, as he slid against the wall into the room.

Paul Somnevausky, who always positioned himself strategically near the plate of teatime cookies, was somewhere midway through his process of selection. He was not a sociable physicist, and yet he never missed the daily ceremony of the departmental tea, approaching the event with his own axiom of choice. It was his method to go after only the cookies with colored sprinkles, starting with those the most heavily laden and working his way down. A first-year graduate student, who did not know any better, was trying to speak to him of the scattering of particles, while Somnevausky, solemn with indecision, compared the sprinkles of a rainbowed cookie with one monochromatic blue.

The long, pale, elegant figure of Philippe Ledoute, wearing his habitual black turtleneck despite the heat, was sprawled out on a low leather chair, discoursing to the small cluster of graduate students at his feet in his dissipated but tireless voice on his subject of choice: Wittgenstein and Bohr and "the axiom of the unsayable."

"Bohr's statement that *the extent to which an unambiguous meaning can be attributed to such an expression as 'physical reality' cannot of course be deduced from a priori philosophical conceptions but must be founded on a direct appeal to experiments and measurements* is essentially isomorphic to Wittgenstein's statement that *the difficulty in philosophy is to say no more than we know.*"

Neither Ledoute nor Somnevausky nor any of the others appeared to see him as he entered the common room, where every day the physicists gathered, in the late afternoon, between the last class and the four-thirty seminar. Undetected, he poured himself a cup of tea and did not disappear but stood against the wall and sipped, and it was only then that Justin looked away from Spencer to see that Samuel Mallach was standing nearby.

For years and years he had taught his classes and then fled to his home. He would have sooner taken a gun to his left temple than taken a step into the faculty lounge, where the physicists gathered in the lull of the late afternoon.

Dietrich Spencer had gotten back only that day from his conference on the West Coast, which had been held at the namesake of the bishop who had so despised the very thought of matter. We are all of us ghosts in Bishop Berkeley's ontology.

"I had not expected it to be such an interesting event. It had promised to be very run-of-the-mill."

There was a story, they could all tell it was coming, and even those arranged around Ledoute gave themselves up to attitudes of more or less appreciative receptivity, everybody marching to Spencer's drum, while Samuel Mallach, against the wall, invisibly sipped his tea, holding the saucer in his right hand and the teacup in his left.

"I was to give one of the two invited talks."

It was an attribute of his, as inseparable from him as his incongruous voice, to point out each indication of his professional high standing. An invited talk is a relative honor, although a negligible one to a man of his stature. And yet nothing else would do than to have it explicitly remarked upon.

"I finished my paper and suddenly, before the first question is even posed, there is a man charging up the aisle, demanding the microphone, which nobody is fool enough to yield him. This, of course, does not deter him in the least. The auditorium where I was speaking was rather large. It looked as though it might have seated five hundred, and it was definitely near capacity. Nonetheless, with only his Mephistophelian energy to amplify his voice, he launches into a denunciation of my lecture.

"It is actually a formal little presentation that he gives, almost sounding preassembled, and the major point of it is that I had viciously and maliciously violated Boltzmann's solution for the arrow of time! I had no idea what he was saying, and quite frankly I felt a tiny bit distressed. I couldn't exactly see what my results had to do with Boltzmann's solution, but when someone is so vociferously denouncing one, it can be slightly difficult to think at all. Apparently, he is a notorious Berkeley crank. I remember only his first name because it is Aristotle, and they tell me he had once been a Berkeley graduate student who had flunked his quals or had withdrawn voluntarily — no one is quite sure — but in any case he suffered some sort of discontinuity and is now a little bit crazy. He surfaces now and then for the sole purpose of formally denouncing a physicist for violating Boltzmann's solution to the arrow of time! He can become, I was told, quite melodramatic, especially after a sufficient number of drinks, on the subject of Ludwig Boltzmann and what he calls Boltzmann's 'fatal vision.' His thesis is that Boltzmann was driven to his suicide by the murderous obtuseness of his fellow physicists, who never grasped his solution to the famous problem. Obviously, Aristotle feels that his genius, too, is going indecently undetected. They told me he only shows up for a physicist he thinks of as a big shot, so that I should take it as a tribute.

"In any case, he is railing against me, and frankly, I'm not certain at this point whether he has a point or not. Some of what he said sounded distressingly as if it might possibly make sense. This is something I've often noticed about lunatics, of whom I have known several: they can sound quite convincing, even compelling, but only for very short periods. Sooner or later, they betray themselves.

"I asked him if he might be a little more concrete, and tell me where, exactly, my mistake was made, and he bellowed out that my calculations are rife with errors, that not an equation has been unfudged. Then, of course, I knew the man for what he was. I knew that Aristotle was a confirmed crackpot . . . since it had been Justin Childs who had done all my math for me!"

He got the eruption of laughter that he was after, pounding Justin Childs on the back, and before Justin could even reach him, Samuel Mallach had fled from the room, teacup in hand. Dietrich Spencer turned his head on his powerful neck to watch the swift exit with an expression entirely inscrutable.

XXI

She is slowly coming toward me, the little barefoot girl in the long white nightgown.

I follow her down the long unlit corridor, and she inches the door open and the bed is empty, its covers undisturbed, and she turns and goes from room to room, so many rooms, I am behind her at every step, and each room is empty. I can feel the pitiful tremble in her child's body, as we go down the treacherously swirling stairs, until finally we come upon him.

He sits in the library, staring dully. There is no fire in the fireplace, under the portrait of Carlotta with her oblique gaze. He doesn't raise his eyes, or move a muscle of his face, as we come and stand before him.

— *Daddy*.

She stretches out her hand to stroke his cheek, dry beneath the eyes. They will not bend their awful gaze, though she calls to him the one word, *Daddy*, the soft sound of it like some too-soft creature dying soft against the glass, *Daddy*, her breath filling it with her own soul, *Daddy*, the soft sounds of it turned to particles of light, *Daddy*, suspended before his inverted eyes that see nothing of the light she makes, *Daddy*, attuned only to the properties of darkness.

Daddy, she says, and I whisper with her, night after night, we whisper, *Daddy*.

XXII

In her eyes there was an articulation of terror so stark it seemed that of a very small child.

She flung the door open before I had placed my finger to the bell, and before she had said a single word, I was frozen icy numb by the look in her eyes.

She had sounded calmer on the phone:

— *I knew this would happen.*

— *How could you have known? How could either of us know? He never goes anywhere near anyone else in that department. How could one possibly have known he would suddenly take it into his head to go to one of Spencer's infernal teas?*

— *Have you spoken with him since?*

— *No. He escaped before I had the chance.*

— *Escaped?*

— *Turned on his heel and left. He was still carrying the teacup and saucer.*

That particular detail struck me as singularly ominous. She must have thought so too, for I heard her sigh into the phone, the sort of jagged sigh that comes after long crying.

— *Where is he now?*

— *He must be on his way. Where else would he go? I'm sure he'll be home any minute.*

— *Oh God. Please, come. No, don't. No, do.*"

She hung up.

When I arrived at the home on Bagatelle Road, Mallach still had not been seen, and Dana's eyes and face had gone awful with uncertainty.

We sat side by side in the library, where Carlotta stared off into her mystic faraway. For a long time, we said nothing, only listening for his footstep on the front stair.

— *Perhaps we should look for him.*

Dana simply shook her head and listened.

— *What exactly are you afraid of? What exactly do you think that he'll do?*

— I don't know.

Her voice was small and terrified, sounding more like a child's than ever before.

— I don't know. I wasn't with him that first time. I was with my grandparents, I wasn't with him.

— The first time?

She shook her head and listened. The clocks in the house, all the clocks in the house, were chiming the hour. Five hours had passed since I'd seen him disappear out the door of the common room with his teacup and saucer.

— My grandparents came here to take care of me. They'd moved away from here, to Arizona, but they came back to care for me. They once took me with them to visit him. That must have been when he was getting better. They let him come out and sit with me on the grass. The place had beautiful grounds, I remember that. It looked like a park. Before that I'd never been allowed to visit.

— A hospital? It was a hospital?

— Of course. Didn't you know? He was there a long time.

— How long?

— I don't know. I was just a child, nine. Maybe it wasn't really all that long, but it seemed that way to me. It was after my mother died.

She fell into silence for a short while, her lips moving slightly as if in private conversation with herself.

— He loved her so much. My father loved my mother so much. They didn't mean anything, in the end, the fights. He loved her so much.

— Your parents fought?

— Mmm. Well, really my mother. I used to hear her shouting and . . .

— What?

— Crying. He was always quiet, while she screamed and

screamed and then cried. I never heard him answering her at all. And when she died. . . . And then he was gone in that place. When he came home it was terrible, too. My grandparents stayed here with us, past my thirteenth birthday. He was completely incapable of taking care of himself, much less of me. I don't know if he'd had shock treatments. I've wondered because of all the damage to his memory.

— You've never asked him?

— We never talk about that time. But I don't think he did. I don't think he ever would have submitted to shock treatments. He would have been too afraid of what harm they might do to his capacity to think, to do physics. But, of course, he was heavily medicated. He's still medicated. He has to take his pills for the rest of his life. Maybe it was all the medicines that made him the way he was when he came home.

— How was he?

— I can barely describe it. He was empty. He was absolutely empty. I would come down in the middle of the night and find him sitting here, staring with eyes that looked like a dead man's. Oh God! I couldn't bear it if I were ever to see those eyes again. Justin, I couldn't bear it!

She got up and began pacing back and forth before me.

— How could I have let you do it? It's all my fault. I'm the only one who knew the true risk involved! Oh, Justin, how could I have let you do it? What was I thinking? How did I let myself get lulled into such a state of insensibility that I didn't protect him when I could have? I'll never forgive myself, never!

Just then we heard the key in the door and Dana started up and ran to fling it open.

— Daddy!

I could hear the low murmur of their voices together, for

a long time, as I sat in their library and waited, and their voices faded and I sat looking at the image of the vain and empty woman who had brought Samuel Mallach to the brink and then hurled him over, and made her daughter motherless at nine.

Which circle of hell was hers, I wondered, which circle of hell for Carlotta? I stared up at her, to try to see the truth of her. I heard their voices coming from the back room, where we did our work, and I stared up at the treacherous wife and mother.

— *There was someone else with her in the car.*

— *Who? Was it you?*

— *No, not me, and not my father. Someone else. I don't know who. A man.*

I saw it, quite suddenly: that long and brutal stretch of scar of the man whom she had called her uncle Dietrich.

— *It's all right, Justin.*

She came back into the library, her face and voice restored to her, her world and mine restored.

— *It's all right now.*

And she seemed almost to be laughing.

— *Daddy was angry, of course, but it's just good, healthy, justifiable anger. He said he was going to give us both a serious spanking in the morning. He's taken his pills and he's gone to bed, and I think it's all going to be miraculously all right.*

And she was laughing now, truly and joyfully, her world and mine instantaneously restored.

Above her head, Carlotta stared. A new suggestion of fear had crept softly into her gaze . . . for I had found her out.

XXIII

Only the memory of light can draw it here now, immobilized by love, drinking in memories of long-gone light.

It presses hard against the deadened glass that has gone opaque with too much darkness. Crush it, and it goes instantly to ash, a vastness of longing contained in smudged ash.

Even embodied, it was a thing that could barely sustain the metaphysical motions of love, the blisses and the terrors. How then can it endure love in such a form as this?

What thing am I, what thing?

I have answered, may God have mercy, how I have answered.

I am a thing that loves.

XXIV

— I think it's all going to be miraculously all right!

We climbed the swirling stairs and went, our arms tight around each other, down the long unlit corridor that led to Dana's room.

— *He's gone to sleep. He took his pills and went to sleep. He'll speak to you in the morning.*

— *Do you think he'll yell at me?*

— *Oh, Justin. You're such a little child! Justin the Child, crown prince of quantum mechanics.*

— *And you are the princess.*

— *And he is the king! My father is the king!*

She had said that I was a child, but I felt that it was she who was the child, that she was as young as I was grown-up. I knew something about her life, a hidden variable that she couldn't have observed and would never infer, and I wouldn't tell her. He hadn't told her, so I knew that not to tell her must be right.

It was right to let her love her dotty mother, even with an erroneous, irrational, infuriating love, because it was her mother, the only one she would ever have. I repeated this over and over in my head, as if it were a fundamental truth, because it was.

I paused in the corridor, outside her bedroom door.

— *Perhaps I shouldn't stay over tonight. If he's still angry with me, perhaps tonight it would be better for me to go.*

— *Don't be silly, Justin. You know that he doesn't mind your staying.*

— *It's what he wants. It's what he wants, isn't it?*

— *Mmm.*

— *It's strange.*

— *Strange, yes. It's strange.*

She smiled at me, the radiance slowly coming, coming. Onto the bed she stretched herself out long and sighed.

I stood and watched her, enchantress of the world, as slender as a lotus stem, the radiance slowly coming. I had only to watch her stretch herself out long and sigh, and reach her hand out, palm up, to feel the radiance coming.

It was this that he had meant.

— *Strange, yes. It's strange.*

— *I understand it, though.*

— *What do you understand, Justin the Child?*

I came toward her now, and kissed her open palm, mouth laid on that other mouth that leads to bliss. It was this that he had meant, this search and this: the shuddering knowledge.

— *What do you understand?*

We lay quiet after long love, entangled in the moments before daybreak.

— *What do you understand, Justin?*

She murmured it against my shoulder, barely audible, the slight hiss emerging as it often did when she was tired, her legs still wrapped in mine, so that I didn't know which were hers and which mine. Our world had been restored to us and reconfigured, with something fundamental in it fundamentally now changed. Perhaps, I thought, reaching for the terms of the quantum condition of collapse that consumed us: perhaps it was no longer even meaningful to raise the question of our distinct psi's now at all.

— *Tell me what you understand.*

She said it with a slight press of insistence. I moved away to look at her. She was softened by our love, all things about her soft, her eyes half sleeping and ready for her dreams, and I would lie awake and watch her while she slept. Was she still as beautiful as before? I could no longer tell, I loved her far too much, too much. Only the psi of our union is defined now, I was thinking, free-falling into poetry, into metaphors and dreams, become at last a physics-for-poets nonpoet, loving her far too much, and so I told her.

— *That afternoon last winter when he and I went for a*

walk and you stayed home. It was the day that we had proved the bizarre efficacy of knowledge.

— Mmm.

She lifted her chin in the gesture that told me to continue.

— *He told me about Erwin Schrödinger, how his wave mechanics had poured out of an ardent love affair, a secret Christmastime tryst with a woman whose identity has never been learned. He thinks love like ours can add a fire to the understanding, Dana. Did you know that? Did you know that he thinks I do physics here in your bed? He means to get the physics out from me!*

I had meant, I think, to laugh when I said this, but my tone could not have been further away from ridicule. I spoke the last words with an excitement that took me by surprise, only fully realizing, when I finally spoke the idea aloud to her, how proud of it I was: the great chain of knowing passing from God through Galileo and Newton and Einstein and Schrödinger and Mallach and me.

She turned her eyes away, but not before I had seen their look.

— *Tell me, Dana!*

She was turned toward the wall, her knees drawn up beneath her chin. I grabbed her knees and swiveled her back with such a lightning quickness that I heard the joints of her protest and the rest of her followed unnaturally after.

— *Tell me! You know that you can't keep it from me!*

She stared up at me, her eyes no longer soft, but full of their light blue light, a shade of blue I'd never seen before that autumn hour on the stairwell landing, when I had been, with all the certitude of well-formed instinct, afraid.

She said it softly, but with a measured clarity and charge.

— *From me, Justin. He means to get the physics out . . . from me!*

XXV

"Mallach, you say? Mallach? Did I hear correctly, young lady, that your name is Dr. Mallach?"

It is the faculty Christmas party at Olympia College, held in the space they call the Tower Room. It is the first faculty Christmas party that Dana has attended in all the years and many places that she has taught, crisscrossing the country from one college to the next.

The room is one of the college's finest, reached by spiral stairs that ascend from the department of religion.

Modest Olympia is rather proud of its Tower Room, whose proportions are baronial, as Miss Wyndham might say, with walls of rich mahogany, chairs and couches of green leather bordered with brass studs. And there is Miss Wyndham's understated elegance as well, quietly entailed by a few Oriental rugs and parchment-shaded lamps and latticed, leaded windows that face west. The sunset of the early-darkening season stains the glass ecclesiastically, adding a touch of the churchly to the clubby scene, all gone gaga on eggnog, so that no one remarked her quiet entrance.

She stood for a few long moments just inside the door, trying to patch up her jagged breath and wait for the room to stop its spin. Her limp has gotten more severe in the last few months, and the climb up the steep spiral stairs had been accomplished with pain. Three times she had stopped, and three times winced.

She is wearing knee-high boots, a pair of woolen trousers, with two sweaters piled on, and over it all, a long gray coat with a prim black velvet collar, and she thinks that she will never feel warm again.

The snows have covered Olympia for four weeks now, the steep road leading up to the campus plowed three times a day. Down the road, in the buried little town, icicles shaped like great crocodile teeth hang from the house, white on the bottom, with bumpy green shingles on the top. And beside the golf course, in an even tinier house, looking as if it might be made from gingerbread, a poet daughter greedily grabs at the few brief hours that her ancient father will be away at the faculty Christmas party, and is playing Mozart on the cello. Her head is bent low, so that the long hair, streaked wide with white, falls across the instrument that is making music so like the play of light on water.

Dana has felt, since the hard winter arrived, that she barely retains the memory of warmth, and she knows that she will never be warm again. She stood there close to the door for at least ten minutes after entering, unnoticed by any of the tippled faculty, trying to recover the breathing that had been wrung out of her by the climb up the spitefully twisted stairs, the searing jabs awakened in her chest, where the murderous moths are silently swarming in the lump that grows in her right breast.

She knows that they are swarming and she looks away. It is her intent, for now, to look away. She realizes that if anyone knew her cold resolve, they would think her mad, but there had been no deliberation required at all in her decision to look away.

She stood by the door inside the Tower Room, calmly waiting for her breathing to return, for the world's fierce spin to still itself slowly, and when this finally happened she was able to make out some reassuringly familiar faces, the gentle wave of recognition slowly passing over her face.

There, beside the back wall, were two physicists from her department, one of them her special friend, Wallace Low, chatting together with an engineer, and several chemists, all of them composing one cluster, the scientific one, in the crowded Tower Room. The Olympians are scattered in departmental clumps, sipping from plastic cups of eggnog, growing dignifiedly tipsy.

The cluster of her friends was bent down to a small being taking up very little room on a great winged green-leather chair. One could sit a whole other full-sized person beside him.

A child, it seemed at first, its feet in massive black shoes planted firmly on a patterned rug. In proportion to the tiny body the head seems monstrous, its hair once yellow, then white, now yellowing again, no child at all but an aged man, and I know his name:

It is Professor Cock-A-Doodle-Do. It is Cock-A-Doodle-Do, still crowing, or, in any case, breathing. His sunken eyes, magnified behind their lenses, rest on the sagging pillows of fleshiness just beneath them, and his cheeks are like the pleated skirts that Cynthia would carefully iron with her stubby but capable hands. Bent down over the ironing board, she would look up when I entered the kitchen, and she would smile, as Josiah Krebs now looks across the room and smiles, with a gnome's conspiratorial glee, looking straight at me.

The others were bent down low to him, trying to carry on a crooked conversation, but they straightened as soon as Dana, still chilled to the bone, she will nevermore be warm, approached. Wallace Low reached out his hand to take hers, icy and shaky, and pull her in, making rather a silly spectacle of introducing her as the newest member of the department. "Wildly successful, her classes are sometimes oversubscribed. We are actually inducing some students — or should I say victims? — to major in physics."

The others were gone enough on eggnog to laugh uproariously, all except the suddenly wide-awake gnome.

"Mallach, you say? Mallach? Did I hear correctly, young lady, that your name is Dr. Mallach?"

His eyes, vitreous behind the bottle-thick lenses, are uncannily lit, and Dana is still trying to quiet her shivering. Wallace Low, looking solicitous and in love, has run to get her some eggnog, and she gulps it gratefully.

"Do you spell it M-A-L-L-A-C-H?"

She nods her head yes, verifying the spelling of her name, distracted still, so that she misses seeing the strange reaction she has produced in the ancient man perched on the green winged chair.

His feet in the orthopedic clogs are kicking back and forth, and he stares like a lover or a lunatic up into Dana's bloodless face.

"Do you know, young lady, that's a very promising name for a physicist. M-A-L-L-A-C-H." He spells it out again.

Dana turns her attention, from the cup of eggnog she has been trying to down as quickly as possible, to the man with the mothy skin staring bug-eyed at her from below. She stoops down to him in her long gray coat, which she has not been able to bring herself to remove, despite the gallant attempt on the part of Wallace Low. He had taken her free hand between his two great warm palms to try to warm it, but now he must relinquish her as she stoops precipitously down to the shriveled man of science, so improbably alive, and brings her face, so thin and chalky white, near to his, disregarding his old-man breath, her eyes suddenly startled into a wonder of attention.

"I know of another physicist who was named Mallach, same spelling. For some reason, nobody seemed to pay him very much mind. He wrote a grand paper on quantum mechanics. Nobody seems to have read it but me. It was a grand thing that he did. He answered all my doubts, and I had quite a few, I seem to remember. I can't remember any of the details now, but you ought to look it up for yourself someday. After all, young lady, it's your name."

And oh to see her smile! It wrings the soul to see her smile so, the full range of her rapture all at once rekindled by the obscure words of praise spoken by a man whose greatest pride had been the laying properties of his Rhode Island Reds and the music of his fairy-sprite daughter.

It wrings the dreadful pity to see the light that comes into her face, the girl of furious light once more, so that she is utterly ravishing to the sight.

XXVI

And ravished still, to see her eyelids shiver over dreams.

I would not move a muscle while she slept, her sleep so easily disturbed. At some mysterious signal she would stir, sit up, becoming instantly awake.

— *Justin Childs.*

She sits up straight now in her bed.

And ravished still, I move toward her, she looks at me, she doesn't turn away.

The mysteries of the particles and waves, the gnostic fields of knowing that link each to each: all must merge in Einstein's truth, in the immense structure of symmetry merged, but who can see it, who see how?

Infinities arising where they are expressly unbidden, so it is that she has been battling against infinities that will not be gone. It is the wild infinities that hold the last of the formidable problem, of merging the mysteries of nonlocality and the vast, spread stillness of objective time.

I had asssured the two of them that my math would tame the infinities back into place, that I had located the form that would fit around the densities of their vision. If we could have worked it out so that it was beautiful, so that it was diaphanous and lit, then we would have known. And then we would have told an astonished world.

And ravished still, I move toward her.

One or the other of the physicists was always summoning me to bring the pure fire of math down to them, to place it into the cold substance of their science, though Dana would often grow impatient with my abstractions, waving her hands and turning away.

— *I need to feel the physics here inside of me, in my own muscles. My father was the same and Einstein too. Did he tell you that?*

— *Yes. We walked around a frozen pond and he danced some physics out for me. It was a dance of ecstasy he* danced, the day that we three proved the bizarre efficacy of knowledge. You dubbed it that.

— The knower and the known, always susceptible to each other's influence.

— He told me how you had danced out the progression of the gyroscope when you were a young girl. Not Bohr or Planck or Born, Pauli, Dirac or Heisenberg. Not even Schrödinger. They none of them felt it in just that way. Dana feels it, too, he said, that you know, and I said yes.

— Yes.

And ravished still, I move toward her.

She is sitting straight up in her bed, on the night table the sleeping drafts and the teacups stained with herbal leaves, the halfhearted gestures she makes against the murderous ravages at work in her breast.

We each carry our own designated end within us, our very own death ripening at its own rate inside of us. We carry it in us like a darkening fruit. It opens and spills out and that is death.

She shoves the bedclothes to the side, the down-filled comforters she piles on top of her each night to try to fend off the cruelties of the cold, and, as if she were the young Dana Mallach again, with youth and beauty preserved in her limbs, she jumps lightly to her bare feet, and slowly raises up her palms to me as, ravished still, I move toward her, she moves toward me.

And one must know her face as well as I, one must have been an advanced student of her features through all the years, to see the astonishments wrought in the mysteries of the transformation, her beauty purified, too pure and bright for sight now, for any sight but mine, her body so filled by the beauty of the equations that there is no place in it now left for her.

She sighs, then moves, a vast and hidden motion down inside of her, a displacement deep in her own body, like two ecstatic dancers only conscious of the dance, neither knowing where one soul ends and the other begins, dancing out the mind she's always known was there, the fact of spirit caught in the last equations, with all infinities subdued.

Palms up and she is dancing, and I am dancing godlike in her limbs.

XXVII

They worked through the days, only pausing with the timid approach of the deer.

It was an October of long, hot, summery days, though the earth had tilted, the trees gone to their dramatic shades. Out from the raging colors the deer would come to eat the apples Dana set out daily on the ground for them. Her father loved these creatures, loved it when they drew near. They watched the silent feeding through the large glass windows looking out onto the wooded back.

When the word came, he had felt a knowing panic. Justin Childs stepped out from his classroom, a piece of chalk still in his hand, forgetting to put it down, leaving his few students gaping, for the corridors were ringing with the word from Stockholm, and the word was "Spencer."

He stepped out and heard that it was Spencer and Zweifel, for their work on background radiation of a decade before, completed when he, Justin Childs, was still living within his haze of unimaginative safety, constructing his truth tables for propositions of a first-order logic that had seemed inviolably complete.

The word came down from Stockholm declaring that Spencer and Zweifel's stumblings in the dark had led to a greater knowledge of the cosmic spectacle that had given birth to all the world, and the word rang out through the corridors of the department, in voices that were triumphant or aggrieved, with money changing hands, for almost all had taken bets, from the lowliest struggling graduate student to the other two Nobel laureates.

There was a larger than half probability, according to Justin's desperate calculations, that Mallach would not even hear the word from Stockholm. He taught his courses and fled the campus, more swiftly now than ever since that one brief visit to an afternoon tea.

But before the door was even flung open to him by Dana, he knew it had all changed and it was a different world entire.

"Not now, Justin. Stay away."

She whispered it, a low and angry sound, its hiss unleashed, and her face was barely one he knew, her lips making a cruel shape.

"Just leave us alone. Go away and leave us alone."

She tried to close the door on him, but he held it open with his whole body, if only he had never held it open.

Mallach materialized from behind, his voice the high tremolo of his memorized poems.

"False friend, false friend!"

It was a different Mallach, like some avenging angel beating wings of implacable flame, drawing down a hatred that can blacken out the world, and the high stilted tone of his voice so hideously at odds with the great solemnity of his pose that, hideously, Justin did not know whether to laugh or to cry.

"Must you pursue me as God pursues me? Think again: let me have no more injustice!"

And still Justin could barely restrain the lunatic urge to laugh, he felt half-maddened by the desire forcing its way up his throat, threatening to split him wide open, though he could feel the annihilating breath of those great fiery wings, and Dana's face was a mask to him, her grief and frenzy painting a frightening stranger over her features.

"My entire life I've been betrayed, and you, false friend, are the last and you are the worst, but at least you are the last!"

Against the awful beating of those world-blackening wings, the voice of reason makes a pitiful whine, and so it was, in the thin voice of reason, that Justin whined.

"I never betrayed you. Any work I did that wasn't with you was nothing! It was shallow work, completely shallow!"

Mallach made the mirthless sound that was his laughter.

"Shallowness is the property the world loves best. Only be shallow and the world will love you."

The bitterness with which he spoke these words, the bitterness, so that Justin, hearing it, cried out. He had thought that he might laugh, but instead there rose up out of the deeps, those awful deeps, this dreadful cry of pity, he cried aloud from pity, to see the precise shape of the bitterness that had all along informed Mallach's madness, that had given to his sickness its deathless life.

How much Mallach must have wanted the world's love, with how much terrible passion, to have answered the world's indifference with such a shape of bitterness as this. He must have loved the world quite madly, madly. All along he must have loved, always desperately longing for the world to love him back.

His madness, then, was the madness of love, and that is always a terrible madness.

He had done enough to earn the love of the careless world, he had done more. Yet here he was, a madman, teaching his Physics for Poets to contemptuous children and fleeing the campus with a madman's terrified haste, lest he be confronted with one more sign of how the world would never love the better man, only lavishing its love upon the lesser.

Unworthy world, but still: the only one we have. It is the only world we have.

Justin saw the shape of Mallach's bitterness and wept for him, while Dana with the stranger's painted face was whispering *Daddy!* and tugging like a toddler on her daddy's arm, though he seemed not to notice, his eyes and wings implacable. And would Dana know, would she ever know, that it was for Daddy that Justin wept and not for himself?

And still, the old yammering habit of reason would not be

denied, and so, though Justin wept, he also tried, in the age-old whine, to argue out the merits of his case.

"The prize is for work that Spencer did ten years ago. I had nothing to do with Spencer's getting the Nobel Prize. I was fourteen years old when Spencer did that work!"

"Spencer! Spencer! Spencer!"

Justin did not know this voice at all, it was the voice of the wrathful angel thundering down from on high, and, only seconds before it had emerged, he had seen from Dana's panicked eyes that Spencer's name should not have been mentioned. Three times Justin had spoken it, and now three times the angel had shouted it forth, his eyes in a terrifying glow.

"Consider the crocodile!" Mallach thundered out. *"He is the child of God's works, made to be a tyrant over his fellow creatures, for he takes the cattle of the hills for his prey and in his jaws he crunches all beasts of the wild!"*

Justin trembled, his terror at this raving drying up his tears, Dana tugging and whispering her pleading *Daddy!*

"God has left me at the mercy of malefactors! He has cast me into the power of the wicked!"

Then silence from the angel, no spoken word at all, but the sound of the eyes' awful fire. It seemed to Justin he could hear their blaze.

When Mallach finally spoke again, it was not with the fearful voice from out of the whirlwind, but with the voice of Samuel Mallach, in the bitter voice of his old rage.

"I studied betrayal for years and years and I thought I understood it on a fundamental level, I thought I had seen clear through to the bottom on the subject of betrayal, but no, no, I hadn't generalized to all the conceivable instances. I hadn't considered the case of Justin Childs."

It was the embittered old man and not the fiery angel who spoke now. Justin could perhaps have endured it better to hear the sound of God's terrible messenger pronouncing his name than to hear how Samuel Mallach said it, to hear the hatred compacted dense inside of it.

Justin did not cry out, not aloud, he did not think.

And even so he clung to what he knew, clung to: *every statement is either true or false, and no statement is both!* And so he pushed on, made reckless on his knowledge of irrefutable logic.

"How could the decision of the Swedish Academy of Sciences possibly affect what I've already done? How can their decision retroactively transform me into a monster?"

"Strength resides in the crocodile's neck, and dismay dances ahead of him!"

The words were those of the angel, but the voice was not. The voice came drifting as colorless as smoke.

"You forgave me before," he whined, he whined. "You didn't hold my working with anybody else, not even him, against me before. Why now is it an absolute betrayal?"

"Daddy, Daddy, Daddy . . ."

"How is what I've done been made any different by what was done in Stockholm? How can that have any possible effect on what was *already done?*"

"The arrows of the Almighty find their mark in me, and their poison spirit soaks into my spirit."

"It doesn't make sense!"

"Every terror that haunted me has caught up with me, what I dreaded has overtaken me."

These last ravings were muttered in his old, diminished voice, the wrathful angel entirely departing, the mumble barely breaking the surface into the audible, and Justin could see now how frighteningly pale the old man had become, Dana tugging at his sleeve, and he, quite suddenly docile, following behind, the door on Bagatelle Road left gaping open, as if forgotten, as if all the external world was at last forgotten, Justin left dangling on the threshold, neither inside nor out, neither dead nor alive, but forever watching, as the two of them slowly climb the spiraling stairs.

XXVIII

It was the nighttime journey she had rehearsed since she was a little girl.

She started up in bed a few brief moments before it came, so that when it came, she was fully awake.

Climbing out of her bed and going on her icy bare feet through the house, the pitiful tremble of her body no more now than on all those other sleepless nights, only now she ran instead of walked, and she knew exactly where to go, she ran straight to where he lay.

He was already dead when she found him. There was no question of that. He had put the gun to his left temple and then pulled the trigger.

A shattering noise that shattered the night wide open and left it bleeding on the other side of the glass, lying among the cores of the fruit they had set out for the deer, the death that had been ripening in Samuel Mallach through all the years.

XXIX

The news from Stockholm had thrust a window of the department wide open, and the external world came pouring in.

There were camera crews roaming the hallways, men and women with pens and pads at the ready, cornering physicists to prod from them a punchy line or two on the ultimate significance of the work of the newly immortalized Dietrich Spencer. Justin emerged from his office to collide with a bristlingly beautiful young woman in a tightly cut and bright red suit, its hemline pulse-quickeningly high across her thighs, who glanced up at the nameplate on the door to ask the surprisingly dishy young man whether he was Professor Childs or only a student.

"I'm Professor Childs," he answered her.

"You look so young to be someone so important." She smiled, showing perfect teeth, while at the same time giving the cameraman a little nod, so that a small red light on his handheld video camera blinked on.

"Could you tell me, Professor Childs, whether you agree that Dietrich Spencer's discoveries in physics cast light on the existence of God, as many are saying."

Justin stared down at the stunning young woman, who was nodding up at him with warm encouragement, and he felt correspondingly stunned. The sweet confidence of her nods disposed him reciprocally toward her, and she seemed not so brittle as a moment before, far more limpid and just as beautiful. He wanted very much to answer her in a way that would please her, if only he knew what it was that she was asking.

"God's existence?" he asked her haltingly. "Who's saying that?"

"Well, apparently not you," she answered, her warm smile going out simultaneously with the little red light on the camera, and her face resetting itself. Justin watched her moving off down the hall in the midst of her technical crew, stop-

ping before the door of Ledoute, who popped out instantaneously and proceeded to opine magnificently on cue.

For the most part, the members of the department mildly
enjoyed the distractions invading their halls. Nobody, of
course, positively reveled in it like Dietrich Spencer himself, who stepped into the world's glare so masterfully that
one might have supposed he had been preparing for it his entire life. The systematic charm that he had been practicing
within the academic community for years was now turned
up a notch or two and equipped with a high beam of flash, in
acknowledgment of the less subtle audience that constituted
the world at large. If pretty young roving reporters wanted
him to wax eloquent on the subject of the big bang and God,
then, by God, wax he would, though the cameramen were
careful to keep the snapping left fingers out of view.

"In the beginning there was the big bang, a moment of infinite singularity, into which we cannot probe. Our knowledge
begins at ten to the minus thirteen seconds after ground zero;
only then can we lift the heavy veil and take a peek. All moments before that one are cloaked from our scientific view,
and it remains to others to imagine what lies behind the cognitive curtain: whether it is there that God's hand may be
invisibly moving."

The man's compressed energy was undeniably erotic, titil-
latingly telegenic. He managed to project himself, most especially before the camera, as both sage and rogue, and it was
all splendidly effective. When he spoke, as he did for an in-
depth interview on BBC 1, of the 10 to the 29th degrees centi-
grade theorized to be the temperature of the very young universe, "far hotter than the interior of any star," he somehow
insinuated that there was something primally libidinal in the
cosmological situation, so that a viewing don at Oxford was

motivated to plod over in her creaking men's shoes to her bookcase, there to lay her hand to a reference that Thomas Hobbes had made to the *libido sciendi:*

"A lust of the mind, that by a perseverance of delight in the continual and indefatigable generation of knowledge, exceedeth the short vehemence of carnal pleasure."

Quite.

Justin had not caught a direct glimpse of Spencer since the news had broken over them, sweeping the laureate away on the exuberant wave mechanics of fame. There had been champagne bottles laid out for a week at the departmental tea, but Dietrich had had time to make only one tumultuous appearance there, on the very first day that the word had descended from Stockholm. Justin had not been in the faculty common room that afternoon, having immediately gone to the house on Bagatelle Road, and since that day he had kept to himself, teaching his courses and then fleeing the campus.

The closest Justin had come, in fact, to Spencer, in the ten or so days that had passed since the external world had broken through, was to ride up in the elevator one morning with Spencer's secretary Della, who was looking decidedly prettified and smug, like a husband-proud wife, graciously receiving armloads of the bouquets of plaudits on behalf of her surrogate spouse. Her hair was somehow different — perhaps she had not been a redhead before? — and Justin seemed to remember that prior to Spencer's ascent she had worn glasses.

"Some excitement, huh." She had grinned at Justin, when he had (gallingly) failed to say anything at all to her on how the world had been decisively reconfigured.

Justin had nodded numbly, for he had become permanently benumbed, and she had shrugged her shoulders and hurried away as soon as the elevator doors opened, an enemy now forever.

So it was that Justin was quite unprepared when, in the late afternoon of the late autumn, the laureate himself had knocked at the closed door of Justin's small office.

Justin had been standing with his back to the door, staring out of his window at the grand and Gothic architecture laid out beneath him. A television van that had been parked on a little side road was slowly pulling away, and a little farther down the same road a township police car was just vanishing. Chalked up on the blackboard were the equations Justin had been working on when the news had come from Stockholm, with a little note to the cleaning crew, boxed off in the right-hand corner: DO NOT ERASE!

Today he would return to his interrupted work. He felt a subtle easing in his mind's icy stillness, the tentative life beginning once again to flow, promising the fire that was not far off.

It was so nearly his now to possess, his and Dana's and Mallach's. He would return today to the difficult mathematics, would crack it open to reveal the final form within, diaphanously lit and irresistible, so that Dana and her father would be appeased.

He had no other resources to unseat their unreasonable anger. Logic fell deaf on their ears. He would have to leap into the fire for them, to leap like the ancient madman, summoning all he had in him and even more. He was gathering his strength for the task even now, convincing himself that the solution most certainly lay hidden where he suspected it. For so long as he could be certain that the answer was there, then he knew he could count on his own brain to find it. And then they would love him, they would take him back and be at peace, the three as self-contained as before.

Spencer had entered and closed the door quietly behind him. Justin had turned from the window to face him, neither man saying anything. Justin supposed that Dietrich, too, must be waiting, as Della had, for Justin to offer the appropriate approbatory words. Perhaps he ought to congratulate Dietrich for having discovered God?

"I've some bad news, I'm afraid."

Justin had heard those words before, and he knew exactly what they entailed: the demon logic of the counterfactual let loose once again.

He did not think to question how it was that, of all in the department, Dietrich Spencer had known to single him out as the designated receptor of the bad news. He saw again the township police car, just disappearing down the little side road.

It's both of them, he thought. It's both of them, again.

"Samuel Mallach is dead. He shot himself last night. The police have just been here to inform me."

His mind froze around the first sentence only. He registered that Mallach had died, only that. The second sentence did not enter his awareness at all. He automatically assumed it was a car crash, that was the picture on which his mind seized up. Dana had a car, although her father rarely drove with her. He walked to the university to teach his classes and then home again to Bagatelle Road. It took him approximately seventeen minutes each way, walking at a quick clip, his eyes consistently cast down. He had a curious jittery gait, as if a verbal stutter had been transferred to the legs, extra syllables before each step, but still he always managed to move with relative speed, materializing and then vanishing, like a trail of condensed vapor in a Wilson cloud chamber.

"Only him?"

"What?"

"His daughter?"

"That's right. He has a daughter."

— *Who are you?*
— *Dana Mallach.*
— *His daughter, then.*
— *Yes, his daughter, yes.*

"I haven't seen her since she was a child. You know her, of course."

Justin nodded, knowing by the tense of Spencer's verb that she still lived. He accepted this knowledge with no further reaction to it. He knew: Samuel Mallach had died and Dana had not. He did not even think to question the source and scope of Spencer's apparent knowledge that he was linked to the Mallachs.

Spencer was shaking his scarred and massive head slowly, back and forth, on his powerful neck. He turned suddenly to the blackboard.

"Your work with him?"

"Yes."

"I can't understand a thing you've written there."

"No, it's very new."

"It's unspeakable, monstrous."

Dietrich said it with explosive emphasis, so that Justin was momentarily confused, until the idea came to him that it was not his equations that were being denounced, but Mallach's death.

"Was it Dana who was driving?"

"Driving? Driving when?"

"When he died."

"He died in his house. He shot himself in his house. Actually right outside it, in the back."

The words penetrated this time.

"With a gun?"

"Apparently."

"How did he come to have a gun?"

"It seems he owned one, incredible as that seems. It wasn't like Sam to be so practical. Who would ever have believed he even knew how to load it? He didn't even know where the fuse box in his house was located." He shook his head again on his powerfully thick neck. "I would like to speak with her, with Dana Mallach. I can't go to the house. I promised him I'd never set foot in it again."

Spencer stared at Justin for several moments, his eyes boring into Justin's, although Justin could not keep his own from straying to the place of the long, pale scar. Spencer waited several long moments, perhaps giving Justin the chance to ask a question, as a good professor will do when he has said something that demands clarification. When Justin remained silent, Spencer continued.

"I would like to meet with her. I want to speak at the funeral. It's fitting as the chairman of his department, but I have reasons that go beyond that. But I must speak with her first." Again he stared into Justin's eyes. "Ask her if she would come. Bring her to my home. Do you have a car, Justin?"

"No, but Dana does. Dana has a car."

"Just so long as you don't let her drive, Justin. She'll be too shattered to drive herself." It took a few confused moments for Justin to identify the maddeningly familiar noise as the softly snapping fingers of Dietrich's left hand. "I should never have let Carlotta have the wheel that night."

There it was, then, Justin thought: the final verification, almost gratuitous by now. Justin felt as aloof from the empirical proof as Einstein was said to have been when they brought him the data that had been observed during a solar eclipse, showing that starlight is bent when it passes by the sun at precisely the angle predicted by general relativity. Einstein had already known, and so had Justin. The actual eclipse of the sun was unnecessary when it came. He had known, without being told, and known, as well, to keep his knowledge to himself, because Carlotta Mallach, as unworthy as he had always known her in his deepest heart to be, was the only mother that Dana Mallach would ever have.

"I need to know something from you, Justin, before I see her. I need to know if she knows about her mother and me."

"I don't think so. No, I'm almost certain she doesn't."

"But you do. He told you?"

"No. Never."

"Then how?"

"Inference to the best explanation."

Dietrich Spencer smiled grimly.

"You're a good scientist, Justin. As good at empirical inference as at mathematical deduction. I think some sell you short." His smile evaporated, leaving behind only its grimness. "And did your inference to the best explanation include the fact that Carlotta and I had informed Sam that night that she was leaving him? We were going to come back in the morning and collect the little girl. We had just left him, had almost arrived back at my house, when Carlotta suddenly turned furiously against me. It was completely irrational. The entire scene was incoherent, surreal. She made it sound as if, were it not for me, she and Sam would have lived happily ever after. It was, I suppose, her feelings of guilt that were speaking. She suddenly found she couldn't bear the burden of her decision. Carlotta was never a strong person. Behind all her poses, the truth of her was something entirely different. I don't think I had fully realized that until that night."

Dietrich Spencer had kept his eyes fixed on Justin's face. Justin could not guess what it was that the man was asking of him, for he did seem to be asking something of him. It was difficult to hold that gaze, to keep from looking at the fright-ful scar. It was impossible.

Justin turned away from Dietrich Spencer's fixed gaze. He looked at the blackboard and suddenly walked over to it, picking up a piece of chalk and replacing a minus sign that had inexplicably been rubbed out.

XXX

— How dare you look at me like that!

There is a noisy fire in the grate, its melody of warmth and well-being incongruously playing in the background, and above the mantel hangs the portrait of the mother and her child, signed by the deceiving *génie mal*.

— *You think you can play God with all of us! You think your selfishness is a law unto itself!*

The artist of the portrait that hangs a few feet above her had flattered her quite shamelessly, superimposing on her a substance and significance, the steady glow of self-possession, so that the real woman looks like a poor preliminary sketch for the portrait that hangs above. Inference from representation had gotten her all wrong, imputing the imperiousness of imaginary powers, all wrong.

Blond like her daughter, blonder than the portrait, her hair is piled high on her head, and she looks, feature for feature, not unlike the woman her daughter will become, though there is a quality more assertively womanly about her, more voluptuous and almost louche, in the pose that she holds on her black high heels, the thin straps around her ankles aglitter with tiny stones, the same glitter dangling from the jewelry at her ears, with one hip jutting outward in her narrow velvet skirt, and on top a filmy blouse, embroidered with all the colors of a winter's sunset, which opens low on her revealed chest, where she is breathing hard.

She is beautiful, though not so beautiful as my Dana, neither in spirit nor external guise. But yes, the mother is beautiful, and touching, too, she touches me, so tentative and bravely scared, Carlotta Mallach.

— *How dare you play the wronged husband! How dare you!*

And who would ever have inferred from the poise and presence of that portrait, the utter pathos of her thinly quavering voice, the vertical lines of frustration on her brow, the tremor in her vibrantly colored lower lip?

The artist has been most untruthful in rendering her eyes, which have more daze than depth, though perhaps she is very drunk, perhaps the daze and the watery gaze and even the wispy voice derive from drink, for one sees it now that she is observably drunk, and the tones of her voice have the shrill brittleness that the weak-willed grasp for when they must force themselves into ill-fitting defiance. So that even now, in her high moment of denunciatory drama, she sounds more a tinkle than a peal, and her eyes flit and flutter like moths that have come to die against the glass.

— *You thought that the two of us would never dare to feel anything on our own, anything that wasn't useful to you.*

— *Carlotta, please.*

Dietrich Spencer is sitting in a high-backed chair placed near the fire, looking so intensely miserable that he seems a crumpled version of himself, his pale eyes eloquently expressing the desire to be anywhere but here.

— *Carlotta, please. It isn't necessary for us to make it worse than it already is.*

— *I'm not making it worse. Or maybe I am. Goody, then. Goody gumdrops.*

She laughs and claps her hands together, her affectation of some gruesome gaiety intensifying the deep distaste in the one man's face, as if he were expectorating bile, dropping his eyes again, his head slightly forward, so that the firelight flickers on the glabrous skin of his skull, while the other sits crocodile still, his eyes like stones, his head several inches above Dietrich's, untouched by firelight, in the other high-backed chair, placed in perfect symmetry on the other side of the grate, one leg crossed neatly over the other, around which he has basketed both his arms, his fingers calmly intertwined, his back ramrod straight. And in this uneasy position he is unmoving and stares at her unmoved, his mouth drawn into a line silent on the subjects of sadness and despair and all other shadows on the soul, unshadowed and unmoved, uncannily unmoving.

— *If I'm making things worse, at least I'm making things different, and that's got to be a thrill for me. It makes me feel as if I almost exist.*

— *Carlotta, please.*

— *No, Dietrich! No! Look at how he's looking at me! Look at him!*

— *Look at what, exactly, Carlotta? What is it I'm supposed to see?*

— *Look! Look!*

Her voice has ascended into the region of frenzy now, it is all very difficult to hear, and with visible pain, Spencer turns his head slightly so that he can see the other, who doesn't turn his gaze to him but remains perfectly still, the emotionless expression frozen on his face.

There is a vast amount of fury enclosed in the rigidity. Spencer cannot see into his eyes, as Carlotta and I can see into his eyes.

Spencer looks at the husband obliquely only for as long as he can bear it, for he is dreadfully conscious of his ignominious role here, and his eyes drop with the weight of the indignity of his position before finally looking back again at her.

— *He looks sad, Carlotta. To me he looks like a man who is sad to be losing his wife to someone whom he thought of as his friend.*

Dietrich's voice is as muffled as his physical self is crumpled, so that, whether by intention or not, his characteristic force is well concealed.

— *Oh, Dietrich, Dietrich, he's not sad at all, he doesn't know how to be sad, only angry!*

She smiles quite suddenly at Dietrich, changing the incline of her head very slightly, cocking it at a coquettish angle, not subtle but very pretty, and Spencer, though still discomfited, takes note of the angle, he likes her better for it, though the other sits just as impassively as before.

— *Come, Carlotta, it's enough. We've said enough now.*

— *No, I want you to see, I want you to see how he's not capable of sadness, how it's only fury at not getting his way.*

— *Carlotta, hasn't he a certain right to be furious? Really, Carlotta, doesn't he have the right?*

Spencer's voice has gone over into pleading, the whining voice that reason makes.

— *What right? He's the one who told me I was to become your lover, that I had to have my own lovers just as he has his, those stupid little girls of his. And Dora, our own housekeeper! Really, Samuel, Dora! And now he plays the wronged husband because I'm going to leave him! Now he wants to make me feel guilty, Dietrich, because I can't stand to be with him any longer, because I can't stand to play by the rules of his absolute selfishness, because I can't stand the very sight of him! Oh, Samuel, if you only knew how deeply I despise you!*

— *Carlotta, it's enough.*

Weary, weary tones from Spencer, one would not guess the force he holds within.

— *No, it's not, because look at him! Look at him! Dietrich, can't you see him? There's no hope at all for us if you can't see him.*

— He looks only sad to me, Carlotta.

About Dietrich's tones there can be no doubt. He sounds a very elegy.

— Sad? Never, never! Ask him!

Spencer only shakes his head, his eyes cast down.

— All right, then, I'll ask him. Are you sad, Samuel? Are you sad that I'm taking our daughter away in the morning, that I'm leaving you for Dietrich? Or have I already served your purpose well enough? Have you gotten enough science out of all the misery and confusion?

— Carlotta, please.

— And if you have, Samuel, then what I want to know is, what I really want to know is, was it worth it?

Dietrich Spencer looks over at Mallach for a few brief seconds, and then down again at the gleaming dark wood of the floor, alit with the reflected radiance of the fire, such an inglorious role to play in the uninspired geometry of the three-sided polygon.

— Sam, please.

Carlotta's voice has quite suddenly lost all its edge, and she droops with supplication, one sees with how much effort she must have fortified her former pose, with how much effort and with how much drink, and she speaks in low and urgent tones.

— Please, Sam, please. You know I didn't mean it when I said I despise you. I only wish that I could despise you! But I have to go, you must understand me, I have to save myself!

She is infinitely pathetic, and it is infinitely hard to take this in, for she is the sort of woman whom my mother had reviled, enunciating obscenities in her girlishly sweet voice, coldly applying even the word that provokes the profoundest atavistic revulsion. An insubstantiality heavily dusted with the seductions of beauty, lacking susceptibilities to the sub-

tleties of the cosmos that had moved the inner spheres of unbeautiful Cynthia, and yet, even so, inspiring a man on the
order of Samuel Mallach to declamations of incoherence
beside a frozen pond. The injustice had smarted intolerably,
so that my mother had worshipped beauty in its every form
except the feminine.

Mallach shifts his eyes at last away from the abject figure
of his wife, his gaze on Dietrich Spencer, who only now can
see the contents of Mallach's eyes, how they burn with the
cold angelic blaze. No word more is spoken between any of
them, and only Samuel Mallach is left sitting there, the fire
still crackling on fondly of warmth and well-being. It makes
a ghostly music in the freezing silence of the room.

— *And was it worth it, Samuel Mallach?*

— *You know the answer to that as well as I do, Justin
Childs.*

— *We never really knew anything at all.*

— *Nothing, nothing at all.*

— *And the essential fact?*

He bends his gaze at last to merge with mine, and in the
clarity of his light-streaming eyes I can at last unravel the fury
of the passions that we are given to live.

The one eye's message is of the eros contained in the
thought, injecting its fire into our yearning to know. And
in the other is the knowingness that comes of love. We are
things that would know and we are things that would love,
and oh how fused is that entanglement, how fused and fierce
and forever in our entangled passions.

— *Of course, Justin, of course the essential fact.*

XXXI

She seemed so singularly calm he hardly knew what he ought to think.

When he called for her, at the house on Bagatelle Road, she came out calmly, spoke to him in measured, quiet tones, turned carefully to lock the door behind her, keeping her ring of keys in her hand.

"It's all right, I'll drive," she said, and he quickly agreed. He had a license, it was a requirement for graduating from Ionia County High School, but had hardly driven at all in his life, so that he would not have known the gas pedal from the brake, and she was exceedingly calm, he knew her moods so well and she was calm.

They were going to see Dietrich Spencer at his home. He had told them to come to his home. He lived a few miles outside of town, and Dana knew the way, she said. She said she knew exactly how to go.

"It was you who destroyed him," she said, though she said it calmly, never taking her eyes from the road.

But the nature of her calmness, he saw it now, was new and full of hidden dangers. Justin saw that her sorrow had turned to madness, as it had been with her father, and he felt the nausea of dread, for he had learned that there is no reasoning with the sorrowing mad.

There was only one way that he knew to cure the madness of the Mallachs. Her own eyes had gone in search of his, imploring him to stop up the embittered contents of her father's soul, the recriminations that could pour from him and coat him and everything near him with the color of black bile and the stench of old despair. And so he had spoken that night of the formidable problem suspended before them like the fire-spilling mountain of ancient Etna: a leap into the lava that would return them as pure and bright as gods, to live on and on forever.

They would live forever.

He remembered how when Samuel Mallach had spoken

like this, of his hatred and world failure, then the bliss had fled from her face, all the warm colors had bled from her face, and her eyes had gone pleadingly in search of his in wordless language, it was as if he'd heard her speaking directly into his mind, and he had answered her and watched the full range of her rapture all at once restored to her, it came back to him precisely, how it was that he had once been able to stave off the madness of the Mallachs, the world-darkening beating of their awful wings, *the world as it really is after all, the world as it really is*, he had known it with sure instinct, so that when she had turned her imploring eyes on him, he had spoken of possibilities for immensity: the unveiling of the implicate order that would accommodate the universe's irreconcilable truths, with all things suspended in the vast and still geometry of light.

So he understood and so he gathered up all the faculties of his mind so that he might know how to say what he must say to her, as she sat beside him in the late afternoon, steering the car easily around the curves of the tree-shrouded road and calmly cataloguing the reasons for her everlasting hate.

"It was you who destroyed him in the end. Not my mother, not Dietrich Spencer. You were the one who made life finally impossible for him. Only you, Justin Childs."

"Dana, listen to me. Listen to me carefully. We're very close. Don't you see how close we are?"

"What?" She turned herself to face him on the right. "What are we close to, Justin?"

"We've almost solved it, we're essentially there. The math is still messy, but it's going to all come together now for us very, very soon. We're so near I can feel the fire of it hanging. Tomorrow, darling, or the day after. Some tomorrow soon. It was always you and I, Dana. Your father wasn't really up to it anymore. His day as a great scientist was over. He knew it and so did we. It was you and I, Dana, drawing it out from each other, drawing the physics out from each other as he'd always hoped."

"How dare you, Justin Childs." She said it calmly, though the hiss of it was deadly, filling my name with some noxious ether of sound. "First you kill him and now you tell me that he was expendable. How dare you. You're more hideous than I ever dreamed. Hideous."

"Think, Dana. Try to think logically."

"How dare you."

"Be reasonable, Dana!"

"You're a murderer, cold and simple."

"You call me his murderer?"

"His murderer, yes. His false friend, that's what he called you himself. It was your falseness that drove him to it."

"How dare *you*, Dana? How dare *you*? I loved him! Dana, I loved him!"

The dreadful ascent, the rising up of love for him, for Samuel Mallach, for if there were fathers in science then there were also sons, and I was his.

"Whether you loved him or not, you managed to kill him. You heard him yourself. 'My entire life I've been betrayed, and you, false friend, are the last and you are the worst, but at least you are the last.'"

"I was the one who brought him back to life. You couldn't do it all those years, even though you tried. I was the one who reminded him of everything that he'd lost, of everything he could still regain. It was me, Dana!"

"Yes, it *was* you, Justin. It *was* you. He was alive, he was alive, even if he wasn't all that he'd once been, he was alive, and now he's dead, and you're the one who killed him."

"No, it wasn't me, Dana. Someone killed your father, but it wasn't me."

"What are you talking about? Who is it that you're going to blame now? Hideous." The hiss of it so deadly.

"You're pathetic! You're like some little child. You don't really know the first thing about it. You have no idea what really went on. The night your mother died, she and her lover, your uncle Dietrich, had told your father that she was leaving him. They were coming back to collect you in the morning. That's what made your father the lunatic he was. Everybody knew he was insane. It was the department's kindness not to fire him."

She turned around to face him, and for the briefest moment there was a shudder rising up through her, pulling all her features along with it, so that she was for one single instant a ghastly ugly woman. Not a frenzy-painted stranger, like he had seen tugging at her father. This one was recognizably the same Dana Mallach, but she was ugly.

It passed, and she was restored, though she still stared at him, her hands not on the steering wheel of her car but on her lap, placed very deliberately and calmly and perfectly still, the long tapering fingers of her hands arranged serenely on her lap.

He saw her hands resting there, and knew that there was something fundamentally amiss, for a few long moments, it seemed, until the world ripped itself open into waves of noise and sickening motion, the car rolling over and over, and screams ascending from every direction of the world.

And then it all stopped, the vast waves of it collapsing, with the car rocking slowly back and forth, a gentle cradling motion and the singsong of a gentle noise. The car was upside down, all things going again to calm, though Dana was strangely gone from his side, and he smelled the fumes of battery acid, so great a silence after so great a sound and motion.

And then suddenly a vast explosion of unleashed voices, voices human and inhuman, each flame distinctly shrieking, with paradox abounding even in death, for though he burned and burned he felt that he froze, that though he was blackening he was turning into ice, she had been hurled out from the wreckage and he was caught, his leg crushed somewhere in the mangle of metal, and she didn't move, he saw the fact of her perfect stillness with his dying eyes, her own eyes mercilessly unveiled, inhabiting no warmth of love at all, immobile in her cold, hard gaze.

— *For pity's sake for pity's sake why can't you pity me as I'd pity you!*

— *But I did, Justin Childs. I did pity you. How much I pitied you!*

— *You didn't move. You looked at me unmoving.*

— *I thought that I was dead. I thought that I had died.*

— *Because you had meant to die.*

— *I had meant to die and thought I had.*

— *And meant to kill me, too.*

— *No. My intentions were all for me. I only wanted to follow after him.*

— *To follow after the beloved dead: I know the desire.*

— *I'd wanted to go to him even before that moment. But then hearing you —*

— *The terrible things that I was saying —*

— *It was all that I could think: to get away from you and go to him. I wasn't thinking of your death but only of mine.*

— *You plunged yourself into the fire. You crawled back and plunged your arms deep in to get me.*

— *Too late.*

Few words can accommodate the full dimensions of our mortal sadness, but these two can, and spoken as she speaks them now, they do.

— *I remember the sound of your teeth chattering as you squatted in the grass beside me.*

— *I remember your eyes filling up with emptiness. A mirror of the world no more.*

— *I saw your face the first time in a mirror.*

— *And I saw you in that same mirror.*

— *I thought you weren't real.*

— *You thought I was a painting. I thought you were a ghost.*

— *You believe in ghosts, Dana Mallach.*

— *I believe in you, Justin Childs.*

XXXII

Not far from the links, lives Professor Cock-A-Doodle-Do with his unmarried daughter.

"A golf course right outside our back door, almost. That's what Dorothea had said when she first talked me into buying this little house. I couldn't really see it, when the university was willing to give us a place right up there on the hill. But Dorothea prevailed. Yes sir, that she did. A golf course right outside our back door, almost. Funny thing. I never did much take to golf. Wasn't my sport."

It is the sixth time he has repeated the tale of Dorothea's prevalence and his lack of all interest in the game of golf to a waning Dana. They are sitting side by side on the green-and-red plaid couch, an electric heater making soft hisses in the grate, and though the small room reeks of heat, he is buried beneath a thick brown blanket, and when he offers Dana a corner of it, she gratefully accepts.

The daughter has tendered cups of cocoa crowned with Marshmallow Fluff, her favorite drink, her sweet tooth still, in middle age, insatiable. Her love of goodies has swollen her small frame, the buttons of her purple wooly vest are strained, and there is an invisible wisp of Fluff gracing her top lip. She is no student of her face, her long dark hair, streaked with wide bands of white, is pinned back with green plastic ornaments in the shape of bunnies, she has no vanity.

She has poetry, however. Upstairs, in the little student desk of pressed pine, is a stack of exquisite poems, perfected over the years, until they have been reduced down to bare astonishments.

Drs. Krebs and Mallach sit side by side, sharing the brown blanket, while the daughter sits in a chair across but near, so that if they leaned forward and reached, they could all touch hands, and between them is a low table on which the cups of cocoa are placed, with only the daughter's drunk down, and lying beside the cocoa are the papers emblazoned with equations.

She has tried to explain it to Professor Cock-A-Doodle-Do and he has listened quietly, nodding his massive head every now and then with what she hopes is understanding. She has tried to explain only the gist of it to Josiah Krebs, and his eyes are bright behind the bottle-thick lenses, they seem to glow with a gnomish omniscience so that she takes heart, she takes inspiration, and she speaks brilliantly of the final form, diaphanously lit and irresistible, her strength holding out until near the end, until now the end, the physics deep inside her, a displacement inside her own body.

— *They none of them felt it in just that way. Dana feels it, too, of course. That you know.*

— *Yes.*

And then it is quite gone, the bliss fled from her face, all the warm colors bled from her face, and she collapses into passive weariness, awaiting the final word, prepared to take whatever it is that will come from the little ancient man of science.

"I liked the golf course most of all in the winter when Dorothea and I would just step into our snowshoes and go gliding right out our back door. Funny thing. I never did much take to golf. Wasn't my sport."

"It's very important what you've solved here. It's quite immense, isn't it?"

It's the daughter who is asking, her voice emphatically unpoetical, almost gruff, and with diction rough around the edges. One could never infer from it the susceptibilities and intimations she holds inside, never deduce the astonishments that lie in a drawer upstairs.

She has sat in a quiet rapture, and Dana, concentrating

hard on our equations, has barely taken in the presence of the heavy face suffused with unidentifiable emotion.

Dana turns at the question to the daughter, and sees the eyes alit behind the black-framed glasses.

"Yes, it's quite immense. It was a collaborative effort, though. I hardly solved it by myself. I've sent it out to a few of the leading journals, but I haven't much faith that they'll take it. The approach is so at odds with the orthodox view, they'll dismiss it as impossible, I think."

"The impossible has a tendency to go among us unseen."

"That's why I wanted to explain it to your father tonight. I wanted to be certain that someone other than myself understood it."

"I see," the daughter answers, quiet for several moments, with only the heater hissing. "And who are the other collaborators, if I may ask?"

"My father, who was Samuel Mallach." And there it is still, in her erupting smile and her voice. She cannot say the name without the vast love of him emerging. "Your father knows of him."

"Samuel Mallach, you say?"

Josiah Krebs, sunk low under the covers, gives one sharp decisive shake of his hanging head.

"No, I don't seem to recall any such name. Was he someone from Olympia?"

"No, not from Olympia."

"I wouldn't have known him, then. I've spent my entire professional life right here, young lady. If he wasn't from Olympia, then I wouldn't have known him."

And she is smiling still, contented, a gentle smile for every turn of the gyre.

"It must have been wonderful to be able to collaborate with your own father," the daughter says, leaning forward in her lumpy pants. She has the look of women one sees waiting at bus stations and other cruel places, pasty under the fluorescent lights, worn out with waiting, except for her eyes, their held hue and life and light and sight.

"Yes, it was."

— *I've been thinking* —

— *Yes?* —

— *The wave function* —

— *Yes, Dana, what?*

"There was another collaborator as well. Justin Childs. The form of the solution is entirely his. It's all of his essence. So it's under his name that I've sent it out."

"And don't you care at all whether your name is known in connection with work that's so important?"

"Justin Childs," Josiah Krebs says before Dana has the chance to respond, though I know precisely what her answer would have been. But Josiah has gone quite suddenly to quivering alertness, his great yellowish head snapped erect, and he smiles his most conspiratorially gleeful smile across the room and straight at me.

"Will you be OK out there? It's so inhumanly cold. You can spend the night, you know. We'd both like it so much."

The daughter says it shyly at the front door, as Dana is making ready to depart, smiling still. She had bent and kissed the ancient cheeks, her vein of tenderness struck open, and he, momentarily nudged from the tenseless manifold of his distractions, had fixed her with a hard and scrutinizing stare.

"Mmm. I'll be just fine. Thank you so much, but I'll be fine."

And with the vein of one now opened, and with the other who is always bleeding tenderness, the two physicists' daughters embrace, clumsy with the bulky clothes and unplanned motions, so that the poet's black-framed glasses are sent flying from her nose.

The poet daughter stands at the open door, watching until Dana has gotten safely to her car, and only then does she turn back to her father, still smiling gleefully to himself, uncomplaining of the reckless draft from open doors, and she shakes her head in wonder, while Dana is limping past her car and heading straight out for the links.

The wide night skies are blazingly clear, with starlight falling thick and invisible on the snow.

Her eyes cast down, she limps slowly out across the frozen ground, until she finds a branch that lies half-buried and pulls it out. And with the jagged broken limb, she inscribes her father's guiding equation and mine and hers beside it. She writes the physics in the unruined snow, thinking that she has done what she can, she has done more, imparted it to the Olympian physicist and the respected academic editors, and perhaps there is one among them who will understand.

Perhaps even, it suddenly occurs to her now with one last leap of groundless hope, it will be the physicist's daughter. The look of her comes back to Dana now, the caught rapture of her attention. There had been the light of some sort of understanding in her eyes, perhaps it had been scientific, why not hope, one last time, that it was scientific?

But if not the daughter, then perhaps the father or a learned editor, and if not any among these, then at least it is here, written gleaming in the particles of snow.

— *There are the eight stars of the enchanted ladder of the fairy girl's hair.*

It is Cynthia Rosenthal Childs who is quietly murmuring.

— *And there are the stars that were the thorns in her lover's eyes.*

It is her husband beside her, Jake Childs, who points out

the two dim stars in the northernmost quadrant of Olympia's winter sky.

— *The heart at the heart of the heart is full of pity. There is always pity in the equations.*

It is Carlotta Mallach, softly brushing the snow from her daughter's blue cheek, who is smiling still, contented.

We are all here, lying beside her beneath the wide night sky, murmuring each to each and reticulating stars.

— *In Greek the word for the universe and for beauty are the same.*

— *Cosmos.*

— *And what shall I study?*

— *The same.*

Paradox abounding, the cruel edge of the cold lifting as we stare starward in the snow, the cruel edge receding far from her and far from me: a memory of a memory fallen broken from out of time.

She is breathing softly out . . . and in, ever more slowly, breathing softly in and . . . out, whole minutes in between, with infinities subdued. We lie together, softly murmuring on the links, starstruck and chastened.

— *Come, my children, we'll go for a walk. We'll take a walk while there's still some light to catch outside.*

It is Samuel Mallach, laughing softly, colliding waves of bliss-sweet laughter, sending a gentle fragrance through the brightness of the clarified night.

And with the fingers of my light, the same with which I brushed the darkness from the leaves and tried to tremble forth the hidden otherness of things, I still the fearful shudder of her passing.

She holds her open palms to me and comes. Slender, as a lotus stem, her eyes wondrously unveiled, she comes.

AFTERWORD

In 1952, a young Princeton physicist named David Bohm presented what is called a "hidden variables" formulation of
quantum mechanics. For various reasons, none of them good,
the formulation — and David Bohm — were dismissed. J. Robert
Oppenheimer had been Bohm's mentor, but he, perhaps more
than any other physicist, was responsible for Bohm's being
buried alive. He has been quoted as suggesting that "if we cannot disprove Bohm, then we must agree to ignore him."

Samuel Mallach is a Bohm-inspired character, with virtually
all the fundamental facts of Bohm's life changed, except for his
deterministic model for quantum mechanics and his subsequent
deep betrayal by the physics community. Bohm, who died in
1992, had no daughter — no children at all, in fact. And his
widow is no tipsy seeker but a sober Englishwoman who devoted the better part of her life to her husband. Though Einstein
himself had early on declared Bohm his successor, Bohm spent
the great bulk of his life in embittered obscurity, in his last years
residing in England and teaching at a night college in London.
He wrote in a personal letter: "I have only one strong emotion
left, and that is hatred for the forces that have destroyed so many
human beings, including myself. For relative to what I could
have become, I regard myself as destroyed."

The philosopher of science Paul Feyerabend, who relished the
role of provocateur in presenting the irrationality and small-
mindedness that can seep into the proceedings of science, as into
all else, remarked once that "the fact . . . that Bohm's model was
pushed aside while all sorts of weird ideas flourished is very in-

teresting, and I hope that one fine day a historian or sociologist of science takes a close look at the matter."

Only relatively recently have a growing number of "respectable" physicists begun working with what they have taken to calling "Bohmian mechanics."

The formidable problem of reconciling quantum mechanics with relativity theory still awaits a solution.